# KARMA'S SHIFT

## MAGICAL MIDLIFE IN MYSTIC HOLLOW

LACEY CARTER ANDERSEN     HELEN SCOTT
L.A. BORUFF

# DEDICATION

*To every woman who just wants a little*
*magic in her life.*

# 1

**Emma**

THE COFFEE SHOP IN THE LITTLE OUTDOOR MALL AT THE EDGE of Mystic Hollow had become one of my favorite places to people-watch. The baristas knew how to make a latte, light on the sugar, taste like heaven. And what was more, I had found it easy to tuck myself into a back corner in the shop and go between people watching and reading my latest spy novel.

At least, that's what it looked like to other people. To *humans*. They had no idea I was secretly practicing my magic on some of the worst people in the town. Okay, maybe not the *worst*, but it did seem like this mall attracted an oddly large number of shoppers just looking to unleash their misery on the people around them. I'd never been happier that I no longer worked in customer service though, I can tell you that much.

So, what better place for Karma to have some fun?

And I *did* have some fun.

Like now, as I watched the scene in front of me unfold.

Normally, I'd be getting myself worked up. Angry at the people who thought it was okay to treat employees like garbage. But knowing that the jerks of the world wouldn't get away with it... I wasn't getting angry anymore, I was getting excited.

"You gave me French Vanilla!" the twenty-something-year-old woman was yelling at the top of her lungs, her stilettos clicking angrily on the tile floor. "I asked for Mocha." The horrible woman slammed the drink down on the counter so hard liquid, and even a piece of the ice, sloshed everywhere. "And *you people* want to make more per hour? What a freaking joke."

I don't know what was worse, the yelling, the mess, or the fact that I'd heard her specifically ask for French Vanilla. But it didn't really matter, this lady was the worst. If I was to take a guess, based on her designer clothes, superior tone, and general attitude, I'd say she had never worked a day in her life.

The barista was staring at the woman with wide eyes, but after realizing the woman was waiting for her to speak, plastered on a strained smile and said, "I'm sorry, ma'am. I'll remake it."

"No!" the customer yelled. "I want someone else to make it. You'll probably spit in it."

The poor barista looked like she was about to burst into tears. "I'd never spit in someone's drink," she said in a weak voice. "But I'll get my manager."

I narrowed my eyes and felt that prickling come over my skin, the one I knew meant my magic was working. Sometimes it felt pleasant, usually when I wanted to bring good karma to someone. Sometimes it felt uncomfortable, like when I was trying to punish someone. But when I was just letting the magic go, knowing that everyone near me would get exactly what they deserved, it felt like it did now. Like a prickling that was both soothing, too warm, and almost relaxing all at once. Kind of like sitting by a fire after being out in the cold.

"Hey." A voice from behind the customer made the angry woman whirl around.

"What?" The angry woman asked, planting a hand on her hip, and turning up her nose at the teenage girl behind her.

"Drink this!" The teenager, who had watched the whole exchange, picked up the half-spilled iced coffee from the counter. Then, she leaned over and dumped the whole thing on the rude customer's head.

Literally, the top of her head.

The woman screeched at the top of her lungs as the teen burst into laughter and ran away, dodging people on the sidewalk and disappearing toward the park trail that led all through town.

I hid a smile behind my hand, remembering one of the first times I used my powers to make a drink spill on a woman. But even though I was trying really hard to "act my age" and hide my amusement, the longer the rude customer stood in place, mouth hanging open, dripping with coffee, the harder I found it to hold back. After a minute, I was giggling so hard a snort actually exploded from my lips.

Oh, it was a good day for the universe.

"Still want my manager to make that drink?" The barista asked, looking shocked.

The woman unleashed a string of swear words, turned to leave, and slipped on the floor. The handful of people in the shop burst into laughter, and the woman crawled out onto the sidewalk. I knew I'd just witnessed karma in action, but I also knew it wasn't done. These kinds of things had a way of sticking with people. So, I had a feeling it'd be a long time before that woman behaved like that again.

Leaning back in my chair, I sipped from my vanilla latte and looked out at the outdoor mall. On one side, people were walking along the sidewalk between shops. On the other, the woods that surrounded the town gave a relaxing atmosphere to this little slice of paradise. And because of the nice weather, all the glass doors around the shop had been pulled back, so the airflow could move through unin-terrupted. It was like sitting outside, but with a roof over my head. Not quite on the sidewalk, but with how short the coffee shop was, it was close enough to feel like I was near everything and tucked away at the same time.

A young boy suddenly came exploding out of the woods on his bike. For one second, I was happy to see a kid without a screen two inches from his face. But the next, I noticed the expression of horror on his face and the way he was peddling like the hounds of hell were on his heels.

Some instinct sent me out of my chair and stepping away from my table, with a few short strides I was out of the shop and onto the sidewalk.

Out of the woods behind the boy came a group of three other boys. One of them ran forward and threw a rock. "We told you not to come through our turf!" the little jerk yelled.

*Oh, no. Not on my watch.* I opened my hands and focused on the group of bullies, who were all shouting insults now with shit-eating grins on their faces. An uncomfortable prickling came, and my mouth curled with anger.

"Billy Thompson!" A woman with shopping bags on her arms rounded the corner of the coffee shop and came to stop right beside me, her voice booming through the whole outdoor mall.

The boy who threw the rock flinched and hunched his

shoulders. His eyes went wide, and the next rock in his hand tumbled from his fingertips. The boy on the bike looked between the angry woman and the kid, slowed, then skidded to a stop to turn and watch.

"Hey, Mom," the bully said as his friends melted into the background.

His mom marched forward. "What have I told you about being mean to your little brother? Did I just see you throw a rock at him?"

I grinned and watched her grab the boy by the ear. He was in for it now.

She berated him as she dragged him away from the coffee shop, and I felt my muscles relax. I hoped the boy wasn't a bully because his mom was, but then I pushed the thought aside. That's not how karma worked. It wouldn't try to teach a kid a lesson by tossing him to the wolves. No, I was sure the mom would have consequences and a firm conversation, but the ear would be the worst of it. I had never been a fan of physical consequences with my own son, but then, my son had never bullied other kids.

He wasn't an angel either. But no one was.

I sighed. It was getting late. And if I started thinking of my son, I'd start thinking about his dad, who was probably still a toad somewhere in my neighborhood. And if I started thinking about toad-man, I'd start thinking about the scary note someone left on my doorstep. It was a nice day, there was no way I was going to obsess about all of that right now, even though my heart was already starting to speed in my chest.

With a sigh and a couple deep breaths, I drained my coffee, relishing the last delicious mouthful. It was time to head home.

As I tossed the cup into the garbage can on the sidewalk,

my bladder squeezed, reminding me I was over forty and had been drinking coffee for hours. As much as I wanted to pretend birthing my son hadn't done major damage to my insides, I'd never again be that woman who could rock a concert all night and not use the porta-potties every couple of hours. *Oh, to be young again!*

And then I remembered all the dumb things I'd done when I was younger and grinned. Nah, I'd keep my weak bladder and bad back if it meant I could keep my lessons too. Those were hard-earned, and I wasn't about to give them up so easily.

Even so, this meant I needed a pee break. Pronto. I sighed and weaved through the outdoor mall, heading for the cleanest bathroom. It was a little further from my house, but well worth having a toilet seat cover, paper towels, and a clean toilet.

After using the facilities, I headed down a side street toward my neighborhood. Not only was sitting downtown a great practice for my Karma, the walk to and from had helped me feel like I got a bit of exercise in, especially given how hilly the roads were. As I huffed up the street, going through a stretch lined by woods rather than houses—another perk of small-town living—the afternoon seemed to get oddly dark. I picked up the pace, huffing as I headed up the hill.

The forecast hadn't called for rain, or I wouldn't have come today or at least I would've brought an umbrella. I eyed the sky with concern. It felt kind of strange to watch the dark clouds rolling in so quickly. Had the weather always changed this fast in Mystic Hollow when I was younger? I wasn't sure but I thought it had. Still, it made me feel unsettled when the clouds moved over the sun and darkness washed over me. What was more, the storm clouds made the temperature drop so dang fast that goosebumps erupted across my flesh.

I was going to have to ask the ladies about whether these strange storms were normal due to being so close to the ocean, or supernatural. Now that I knew about witches, shifters, and sirens, this storm felt like it belonged in the "weird stuff" category.

When I was about a hundred feet from the end of the wooded part of my walk, a growl made me whirl around. At first, I could see nothing to explain the unsettling noise, but then I saw two red eyes from the shadows.

My heart skipped a beat. It was probably just a rabid beaver, right? Or an angry raccoon? Or a bunny who's angry at life? I gripped my purse strap and took a step back, breathing hard.

Suddenly, a large black wolf leaped from the shadows. Its lips peeled back, and a roar tore from its lips, seeming to shake the woods around us.

My heart calmed a little, and I sucked in a deep breath to steady my breathing. "How dare you scare someone like that!" I exclaimed, realizing what was happening. This was one of the pack members trying to play a prank and it *wasn't* funny. "You could've given me a heart attack, and then how would you feel?"

The wolf gave another little growl, but it was quieter. Uncertain.

I put my hands on my hips. "What would your mother think of you scaring ladies who are just trying to walk home? Huh?"

The wolf lowered his head and looked up at me with guilty, worried eyes. "You should feel bad!" I exclaimed. "What you did wasn't funny. If I'd thought you were a wild wolf, I might've taken off running, tripped, and broken my leg. And humans don't heal like you lot do."

He cowered more, tucking his tail between his legs.

"That's right. You take yourself home right this instant and stop trying to scare people." As he turned toward the woods, I thought of something else. "Oh, one more thing! You go tell your alpha that you risked exposing your kind for a stupid prank. Go tell him right now, before you even go home."

The wolf let out a pitiful whine, then slinked into the woods.

Served him right. Little trickster. He had to learn.

I carried on, turning onto the road that led down to the ocean and my neighborhood. I lived in the house my parents had owned, with a large lot and a backyard that faced a white sand beach and the rolling waves of the ocean. At least I wasn't heading back to the home I'd had with my ex.

Yes, I knew how lucky I was for such a home.

When I turned off the road and down my driveway, I stopped at the mailbox.

There was nothing but a postcard for Mystic Hollow. It had no stamp, no address, and no return address. Only one thing was written on the back.

*Tick Tock.*

Thunder sounded above me, and a tremble ran through me making my legs shaky. The postcard tumbled from my hand, and I crumbled onto the sidewalk. I knew that handwriting.

The person who knew about my husband, they were here, and they weren't going away.

## 2

## Emma

THINKING ABOUT THE POSTCARD AND WHAT IT HAD TO MEAN, I felt a little lost. Who could possibly know what I'd done to my ex when I'd barely understood it myself at the time? I'd turned him and his lover, girlfriend, affair partner, whatever you wanted to call her into toads in my backyard and run for it. There would've been no reason for a supernatural to be hiding in the shadows of my garden, nor did I believe any human would report seeing something like that. People would just think they were crazy. So, who could have sent me this note and the last one?

Climbing to my feet, I stared down at the postcard again and tried to feel brave. For some reason, even after facing vampires, sirens, and shifters, the situation with my ex shook me in a way I was ashamed of. I felt like I was coming to terms with being betrayed and having our marriage fall apart, yet I still didn't feel too guilty about the toad-thing. If Karma had made it happen, wasn't it what he deserved?

If I ever again met the old lady I'd saved in the street, I'd have to ask her about it. Part of me, and I'm talking more than just a little bit here, wanted to track her down and give her a piece of my mind, but an even bigger part wanted to track her down just so I could ask her how all this worked. I mean, what kind of crap was that to just dump a supernatural ability on someone and disappear. It was like my son coming home and just leaving his laundry for me to do. If I had any say in the matter, it wasn't going to fly.

I trudged up the path that cut through my front yard, feeling a little lost. At least I was coming home to my place in Mystic Hollow with my brother and not my lonely house back home where my college-aged son rarely visited. That was something to feel better about. But when I looked up at the dark house, I groaned, remembering I'd be here alone. Henry had gone over to his girlfriend Alice's house to play some video games. I'd known that, but after getting that postcard it had slipped my mind. As strange as it seemed, I didn't like the idea of being here alone, not at all.

I'd noticed that Alice preferred being over here when I wasn't around, and if I was then Henry would generally go over to her place, well, her parents' place. She was a bit of an odd duck; they both were really. There was something about her though, I knew she was a witch and struggled with her magic, but I knew there had to be a reason she was more open to Henry's quirks than most people were. Maybe it was the fact that he was so straight forward? There was something to be said for people who didn't beat around the bush and maybe as a witch who struggled with her powers, she appreciated it more than most. Worrying about my brother's love life was not what I needed to be concerned about right now though. He and Alice were perfectly happy with one another. I was the one getting creepy notes and postcards left for me.

Grumbling, I shoved the postcard into my purse, my knuckles scraping against the zipper of my wallet as I did, and headed toward the porch, digging for my keys.

"Damn it." I stopped and pulled my purse up higher, trying to see down in it. Why hadn't I turned on the porch light before I left? Oh yeah, because it'd be a bright and sunny day without a threatening note when I'd gone to the coffee shop. Life changed so dang fast sometimes... or maybe it was just my mood that changed so quickly. Either way it could be exhausting. Sometimes I just wanted to scream at everything to stop for a moment and let me catch my breath.

Frustrated, I pulled my phone out of my back pocket and used the flashlight app.

"Bingo!" I finally found them, shoved my phone back into my pocket and looked at my front porch for the first time.

My jaw dropped, along with my keys. Right there on my front porch, next to the door, was a guy completely slumped over. And it didn't take a doctor to see that he was dead. My gaze went from him back to the street. The way he was propped up, over by the railing and the big potted plants, no one would have seen him from the road. Or if they were able to see some of him, he would probably just look like a blanket or something with just his jacket being visible in the dim light. Yet, it seemed crazy to just have a dead person go unnoticed on a pretty street lined with beach houses.

Mystic Hollow was a strange place.

My heart raced. I knew you weren't supposed to mess with crime scenes, but what if the person wasn't dead? What if they were drunk? Yeah, they could be drunk. They could have stumbled home from a bar mid-afternoon in a weird storm, one that I was ninety percent sure was magical in origin, then they wound up at the wrong house, couldn't get in so decided to nap on the front porch.

Totally reasonable explanation.

Didn't explain why his chest wasn't rising and falling, but it was Mystic Hollow. Maybe he was a type of supernatural creature that didn't need to breathe. They existed, right?

My fingers trembled as I reached ever closer for the man's exposed neck, and then I carefully put my finger on his ice-cold skin. After a second, goosebumps rose over my flesh.

Yeah, he was dead. I was touching a dead person.

Biting back a scream unsuccessfully, I lunged for the keys that had fallen from my hand before righting myself and trying to shove the key in the lock, missing the first few times. The metal-on-metal scratching sound was enough to fray my already frazzled nerves. I couldn't stop glancing at the man. My fingers felt strange, icy cold almost like they were remembering what it felt like to touch the man, like touching him had infected me or something. And it was spreading. Of course, that could just be shock as well, the logical side of my brain decided to pipe up when I least wanted to hear it. My heart raced and a scream tried to tear its way from my throat. I was just about to turn and run down the street like a psychopath, when I got my key in the lock, turned it, and threw the door open.

Turning my head for one last look at the body, I screamed for real this time.

Full on bloody murder. In the shower in Psycho kind of scream. Woke up from a nightmare and I lived on Elm Street kind of scream.

There was a ghost on my front porch. I know scary shows have depicted ghosts in a lot of different ways, but this man looked like an entirely grey, slightly glowing, version of any other man. His hair was as dark as his eyes, which was to say, about the color of pitch, and his age was hard to guess, but perhaps he was in his late forties. He drifted just a foot or so off the ground, his pose casual, almost touching the body below him. It was hard to tell much about him since he was slightly blurry, like he had a permanent photo filter on, but it was definitely the guy on the ground. I just had no idea who he was.

I held my breath in an attempt to stop myself from screaming even more. So, ghosts were real too? Perfect. Just perfect.

But could it hurt me? Or was it just going to suddenly vanish into the unknown? Or could it possess me and turn me into a puppet for its own amusement?

"You're in big trouble," the ghost said in a singsong voice, shattering the silence.

I screamed again, just as loud, long, and blood curdling as before, and it was like everything hit me at once all over again. The note, the body, the ghost. It was too much. Running inside, I slammed the door, not stopping for a second. I headed straight for my bedroom and slammed that door, too. Ghosts were real. Ghosts could talk. And there was a dead guy on my porch, oh, after receiving the note and almost being scared to death by a teenage shifter. Worst day ever.

None of this was good. Someone should've warned me about all of this. There should be a handbook. Not for the recently deceased, but for the recently inducted into the supernatural. Each creature could come with a description and state like a football player or a D&D character.

I heard a creak in the house. Heck, could the ghost just

drift inside? Uh, probably. Walls likely didn't stop spirits. That made sense.

Unfortunately.

I yanked my phone back out, hands shaking. I was fairly sure the neighbors would be calling the police after the sounds I'd just made. Not that I cared really, I needed serious help, and I needed it pronto.

# 3

**Daniel**

My nose caught a scent I'd never picked up before. Given the fact that I was deep in my family's land, there shouldn't have been any scents belonging to any shifters, besides my own of course. The wolves sometimes drifted over the property line a little, but I didn't mind as long as they didn't come too far in.

This was different. The smell wasn't a wolf or any other shifter I knew of. Just like humans could hear a voice and know who it belongs to, even if they don't see them, shifters in a town this small got accustomed to each other's scents. I didn't believe there was one among us I wouldn't be able to identify within seconds. Which meant this scent didn't belong to one of the shifters in Mystic Hollow. It was a stranger, one who was cocky enough to step into an unknown bear's territory.

Growling low in my throat, I moved my bulky body and followed the scent with my snout close to the ground. I had to find whoever it was and let them know in no uncertain terms they weren't welcome here.

Other shifters should've known better. They should've smelled me and given me a wide berth. As a bear shifter, we were top dogs so to speak. Wolves might be fast and fierce, but an angry bear? That was a whole other level. Even a pup would scent a bear's territory and run the hell away. Not that I'd be rough with a pup, but I would carry it straight back to its mama, mostly because it'd need to learn the lesson. Not all bears were as forgiving as I was.

But this scent. It wasn't a pup. There was something... off. Something my bear instincts screamed to be wary of. Whether it was the beast within me that was nervous, or the ex-sheriff part of me, I had a feeling that whatever shifter brought this scent would be trouble.

Following the scent took me close to my truck. Which was a surprise. I would have thought even a foolish person wouldn't do more than skirt the outlying areas of my land. But to come close to my home? To property clearly marked, even by human standards. Whoever this was, I didn't trust. Not when they were so clearly willing to flout property lines, legal and otherwise.

When I passed within a few yards of the truck, my sensitive bear ears picked up the sound of my cell phone ringing. I stopped short, trying to decide which should be my priority. I didn't get many calls, so when I did, they were usually pretty important. But this cocky shifter would also need to be dealt with.

Snuffing air out of my snout in frustration, I ambled toward my truck. I'd never make it in time to answer the phone, but I'd call back whoever it was. *Then*, I'd go after the strange scent.

Beside my truck, I shifted back into my human skin,

feeling my bones crack, and my shape shrink. Yeah, I was big for a man, but my bear was bigger. In life, I always felt like I was towering over people, but not just because I was tall, it was as if everything in our world was made for people half my size. But the only time I felt delicate as a human was after I shifted out of my bear form. Then, and only then, I seemed too small for this world.

Opening my car door, I picked up my phone, which sat on top of my clothes on the seat of the truck. I fully expected a call from one of the wolves. Even though their alpha was still reluctant to accept my help after his father's death, he had reached out more lately. Usually by text though, which was the young wolf's way.

But to my surprise, the call had been from Emma. My heart immediately began pounding at the thought. My mind called up an image of her. For so long when I thought of Emma, it was of the shy, young girl I knew before she left, with the kind of smile that made a man feel weak in the knees. Now though, that image was replaced with a better one. Her now, with crinkles at the sides of her dark eyes when she smiled. How she'd touched her black hair in a way that reminded me so much of the girl she had been, a gesture that was nervous and spoke of a woman who had no idea how beautiful she was.

And yet, she didn't exactly call me often. My smile faded a bit. She'd called me for one of two things. Either she wanted to go out on a date, and hopefully that was it, or she was in some kind of trouble. So far, this little woman seemed to be chased by trouble. And as much as I thought I was enjoying my semi-retirement; I'd take any amount of excitement or danger if it brought me closer to her.

As long as she was safe.

I hit the button to call her back and put it on speaker as I pulled on my boxer briefs and began to dress. "Emma?" I asked when she answered. "How are you?"

"Hey, Daniel, thank you for calling me back so quickly. I'm in a bit of a pickle here. Could you come over?"

She sounded worried and upset. My heart pounded even harder as adrenaline pumped through my veins. "Of course. I'll be right there."

"Thank you, uh, hang on." Her voice sounded far away, then she said something in the background I couldn't make out because I'd bent over to yank on my boots. What shitty timing that this happened when I was way out in the woods instead of in town.

Jumping into my truck, I turned around on the narrow path while I waited on Emma to come back to the phone. Usually, I took the dirt paths on my property slowly, but this time I went a little faster. Some instinctual part of me wanted Emma to know that I would be there, any time she needed me, any time she called. Whether it was the bear in me or not, I felt like the most important thing for her to know is that she could count on me. If she didn't believe that, if we didn't build whatever this thing between us was on a foundation of trust, I had a feeling it would crumble.

And this old heart of mine couldn't lose another woman I loved. It'd be too much. And as much as bears were said to be solitary creatures, I knew that would be the thing to finally crush me. Just the idea of her giving that beautiful smile to another man made me grip the steering wheel so tightly that it made a little groan of protest.

"Daniel?"

"I'm here," I called over the roar of the old truck's motor.

"I've got to go, just come as fast as you can, okay?"

"Yeah--"

"Well, not too fast. Drive safely."

My phone beeped when she hung up, so I didn't have a chance to try to question her further. I glanced down at my phone, seeing the red phone icon on the screen seeming to mock me, before I looked back at the trail. There weren't any other cars to be worried about out here, just animals and trees, and the animals were smart enough to stay out of my way. I pressed my foot on the gas pedal a little harder, pushing the truck to the top speed I was willing to go as I wove through the trees.

Damn it. Now I was worried.

I beat tracks getting there, and as I approached the house Emma lived in with her brother, police lights caught my eye. Oh, no. Is this what she called *a pickle*? I was kind of hoping she had something that was too heavy to pick up. Or something broken that needed fixing. A police presence suggested this was more than just a pickle.

But as long as she was safe, we could figure everything else out.

I pulled the truck up into the yard, so I wasn't blocking anyone in, then rushed out to find Emma. Passing a couple of detectives, I didn't know all that well, I went inside and found Emma sitting on the couch, talking to another detective. He nodded at me and stepped outside, knowing that unusual cases were sort of my thing. Along with talking to anyone in this town and getting information, I was often able to find out things from our people that the human officers hadn't even thought to ask about.

Sitting beside her, I took her hand, though my instinct was to put my arm around her. "What happened? Are you okay?"

"I'm okay," she said, but she didn't sound okay. There was a tremble to her voice that I didn't like, one that spoke of fear. The last thing I wanted was for Emma to be fearful in Mystic Hollow.

That instinct to draw her into my arms and hold her tighter washed over me again until I was almost drowning in it, but instead, I just held her hand gently. I had held the hand of many victims. Many people who had come into the station had been scared over the years. I'd meant the gesture to be reassuring. But her hand just felt so small and so perfect in mine that for a second, I was distracted by it. And I never got distracted on the job

"It was awful. I got home and found a body. An honest to God body!" She shuddered.

Uh oh. A body? Murder wasn't exactly something that happened often in a small town. Yeah, there was a lot of bloodshed between the supernaturals, but that was usually taken care of quietly. Bodies weren't just tossed on people's front porches.

This didn't make any sense.

"Any idea who it is? Were there any strange signs?"

Emma's gaze met mine, and she shook her head, but I could tell there was something she wanted to say to me. I sent up a silent prayer that she hadn't gotten herself into more trouble. There was a lot I could help her with. Hell, I'd do anything for her. But this was something else. She was a magnet for strange and troublesome events and that was saying something for Mystic Hollow.

The sheriff walked in and gave me a look I was all too familiar with. It meant something had happened to change the case.

I lifted a brow. "What is it?"

"We identified the body. It's Roger. Beth's ex."

Oh, crap. I was really hoping the dead person had no connection to Emma. Having a body at her house would look bad. But without that, the investigation into her would end quickly and cleanly. Nothing about having one of her friend's exes murdered at her house would keep this thing simple.

"Beth's ex?" Emma's voice sounded small and scared.

I gave her hand a squeeze, wishing I could do more, but knowing it wasn't a good idea with the sheriff watching. The last thing I wanted was to be pushed out of this case and not be able to help Emma, because the police thought I was too close to the possible suspect.

The sheriff turned his gaze toward Emma, who looked stunned into shock. "And it's my understanding that you were yelling at him just a few days ago?"

Oh, man. Having it be her friend's ex was bad. Having it be an ex with whom Emma had been seen fighting? My stomach twisted. If she'd had a fight with the man, she'd be at the top of the suspect list.

At last, she turned to me with big, wide eyes.

She looked terrified. What had she gotten herself into?

# 4

**Emma**

Sucking in a deep breath, I blew on the coffee again, eager for it to cool a little so I could gulp it down. It was the afternoon, but it felt like midnight... like I'd fought a jungle cat and the darn cat had won. Yesterday, I'd spent the rest of the night being questioned by the police until finally Daniel had chased them off to give me some peace and quiet so I could sleep.

Yeah, right. Like that had happened.

I'd barely slept a wink. Every creak or bump I heard was the killer coming back to get me or the ghost about to terrorize me and drag my soul to hell with it, because as callous as it may seem, I had no doubt that was where Roger was going to end up. It should've helped when I realized Daniel was positioned outside of my house in his truck, but it only added to my sense of unease. I went back and forth wondering whether or not to invite him to sleep inside or if that was inappropriate. I mean what if the killer did come back and attacked Daniel because he was there? I didn't think I could handle that, but then I didn't think I could have him sleeping on the couch either. Even though I went back and forth for hours, I ended up never inviting him in. There was some part of me that would have been too tempted to make a move on him if the big man had been in my house, which on top of everything else, would have been a disaster...

And then, this morning when I'd finally dragged ass out of bed, we'd been out of coffee.

Ugh! What a way to start the day. But, at least, not having coffee gave me an excuse to pick some up and head to Private Psych, Beth's private detective business. I was almost in a decent mood until I sat down with my coffee, because the darn cat wouldn't stop glaring at me like I was the one that murdered Roger. I knew that wasn't what she was thinking, but Marble just had this way of making me feel like I was in her space. Which, I guess, I was.

"Enjoying the sunlight?" I asked the cat, who was lying in a patch of sunlight near the front door.

Marble's glare seemed to deepen. "I *was, until you got here.*"

I snapped. "Oh, has it been so hard to sleep and eat all day?"

The cat began to lick its paw, stopping just long enough to say, "With whiny humans disturbing my relaxation. Yes, it has been hard." She let out a small huff before going back to cleaning her paw.

Carol laughed, seeming to enjoy the banter as well as the coffee I picked up for her while I was on my way over. My promise of coffee had talked her into taking a short break from Yarns and Yards. If Deva had been there as well it would have been perfect, but morning was the busiest time of day for her business. Carol sighed and said, "You're never going to have a pleasant conversation with Marble. She hates everyone, except for Beth."

"Beth feeds me," Marble muttered, still licking herself.

I looked at Beth, who was grinning over the top of her own coffee. We were all a bunch of caffeine and sugar addicts, and I didn't plan on quitting any time soon. After taking a sip from her mocha she said, "What? I know the way to a cat's heart."

"I think I'm going to get a dog," I replied, knowing it would insult Marble and not caring.

Marble hissed slightly, then stood, turned around so her butt was facing me, tail high so everything was on display, and sat back down.

"So, should we talk about the elephant in the room?" Carol asked, her blue eyes locking onto me.

I blew on my coffee again and tried in vain to calm my racing heart. Maybe coffee hadn't been such a good idea since my heart already felt like it was trying to break through my ribs. Caffeine wasn't exactly known for its calming effects.

I sighed as my mind spun, remembering everything that happened. Yeah, we needed to talk about it all. No, I didn't want to. As much as I enjoyed the supernatural world, I wasn't exactly excited about the new dangers I was facing. I'd hoped everything would calm down and just be fun after we got Henry back, but it just seemed to be getting crazier. It made my cheating ex seem... less like the worst thing that happened in my life.

Was that a good thing?

I wasn't sure.

At the very least I could now officially say there was nothing special about him. Was I about to forgive and forget though? Unlikely.

"Do you think there's a connection between my ex and the notes?" Beth asked, diving right into the mess that was our lives. Her blue eyes sparkled as she took in every miniscule detail and movement I made, analyzing, and trying to figure out what was going on. She was smart as a tack and put puzzle pieces together in a way I never would have even thought about.

I shrugged and opened my mouth to tell her I had no idea, when a hedgehog I hadn't been introduced to muttered something. Of course, the hedgehog had thoughts on the situation. I was sure the zoo of animals around us, of which there were many, all had thoughts on the current predicament. I just didn't think anything they had to say would be useful. Or very nice.

But maybe I was still mad at Marble.

"Did you have something to say?" Carol asked, sounding way too chipper given the situation.

Great, now we were asking the animals their opinions? I couldn't decide if that was super annoying, or if I just needed more sleep. Glancing at my coffee, I sipped the liquid gold. Maybe after the drink was done, I'd feel more forgiving of the animals. Provided I didn't combust from all the caffeine I'd been consuming. Going back to bed did sound amazing though.

Beth pulled me away from my dream of comforters and dark, cozy spaces as she prodded, "Go on Hedger." We all looked at the hedgehog, sitting on a table as he scrolled through something on a phone. I mean a hedgehog using a phone was just next level bizarre. Who knew they could even read let alone use electronics? I knew it was just Beth's magic, but still. If she videoed this and put it on social media, I bet she'd make a killing. Explaining it would be the hard part though.

"This doesn't look good for Emma," he said in a nasally voice, his little brown nose bobbing up and down as he spoke.

I closed my eyes and tried to respond without sounding as irritated as I felt. "I don't know if there's a connection between your ex and the notes," I said. Even I recognized my voice was super tight.

Not that it shouldn't have been. Someone had been murdered on my porch. I tried to swallow past the tightness in my throat to loosen it but couldn't get it to go away.

Beth's store phone rang, and she snatched it up before the second ring. "Private Psych, how can I help?" She listened a moment before her eyes widened. "Oh, no. I'm so sorry to hear that. Yes, I'll take the case." She turned away, checking her books, and I didn't hear the remainder of the conversation.

The little hedgehog tutted and muttered again, probably something about how I'd be spending my life in jail. Actually, that was what he said. I didn't even want to look at whatever news he'd found online about the dead body and me. Because he was right, it probably wasn't good.

"Sorry," Beth said as she joined me again. "Someone's pet was mauled to death. I agreed to take the case. I want to keep busy." She stared off into the distance. "The news about Roger has thrown me for a loop."

She had to be so conflicted. She'd never wish someone dead, but then again, he was a real jerk who cheated on her for years before marrying her little sister, who was really more like a daughter to her. "It's okay to not be sad," I whispered.

Beth started and looked at me as though she couldn't understand why she wouldn't be upset. "I am sad. But, confused about how I feel. He's gone. *Gone*. No more stress for me. But then, he was with my sister, and I feel really bad for her. I don't know if it would be appropriate for me to call her or try to comfort her." She shook her head and stood. "I don't know. I've got to go investigate that death."

I reached out my hand and squeezed her arm as she passed. "It's okay to feel however you feel. Even if it's relieved."

"Every emotion is valid," Carol added as she set her cup down on the table so she could watch Beth more closely. "It doesn't matter what it is, if you're feeling it, then it's okay. There's nothing to feel guilty about one way or the other. We are all allowed to react to different things in our own way."

Beth put her hand over mine and patted it and glanced between me and Carol as she said, "Thank you, ladies. You're good friends."

She pulled away and went to jot a few more notes down. I just studied her. Beth always had a cheery disposition. No matter what she went through, her blonde hair was always brushed straight and fell around her shoulders in waves. And she always wore light makeup that perfectly empha-sized her big blue eyes and round face shape. But today, underneath that makeup, I swore I saw shadows. And her mouth, that always seemed to be ready to smile, looked forced. Almost plastic. There was too much going on inside her head for it not to be displayed on her face as well, at least to those who knew her well.

I sighed. As hard as it had been for me to find a dead body, and possibly to be the prime suspect in a murder, she must feel like her world had been turned upside down. The much younger sister, Tiffany, who Beth had helped raise, who Beth had sacrificed for over and over again, had just lost her partner. A partner who had been with Beth for years and had two kids with her.

After knowing Beth all her life, I knew her instinct would be to be there for her sister. Everyone in the town hated Tiffany for cheating with her own brother-in-law. The only person she had was Roger and now he was gone. But I hoped Beth had enough self-respect to fight her instinct and take care of herself.

Her sister had thrown her love and support away like trash. She certainly didn't deserve it now. Sometimes family was an obligation that people couldn't walk away from. Tiffany had walked away without glancing back once, as much as I wished Beth could do the same it also wasn't her nature.

Beth looked up, her eyes meeting mine. "I'm okay."

"Are you sure?" I asked.

She nodded, but her eyes shimmered. "Just going to work on this case. And I'll help clear your name. I promise."

I smiled at her. "I can always count on you."

With friends like her at my back, my enemies better be worried. Karma plus a group of witches? We weren't to be trifled with, and soon the murderer would know that too.

## 5

## Emma

When Beth left, Carol excused herself as well, saying she needed to get back to the shop. So now it was just me. And the menagerie.

I drank my coffee and looked at Buster as he slowly walked into the room. The mangy-looking tabby cat gave the white fluff of fur known as Pickle a dirty look, then stopped in the center of the room, glancing around as if he hadn't planned to snag the sunlit spot by the window. When his gaze looked back at me, I swore I saw pity in his eyes.

Did all the animals think I'd be in jail this time next week?

"Stop it," I say, taking another long chug of my coffee, while watching him over the brim of my cup the whole time. "It wasn't me. And we'll clear my name."

He couldn't answer me now. It was Beth's magic that helped him talk. When she left the room, none of the animals could verbalize. In some ways I was relieved, I wasn't sure I wanted to hear what Marble had to say when

Beth wasn't around. Buster was usually a little more pleasant, but they were both cats, so they both had egos the size of Texas.

The cat simply blinked at me and looked away. His pupils had turned to slits in the bright light, but it made him look like he was even more done with me than usual. No doubt since he couldn't talk, I wasn't worth his time. Yeah, well, maybe I didn't want to sit here and talk to him anyway.

I need to shake out of this mood!

I finished my coffee in a hurry, feeling awkward in the room full of silently judging animals. Even the bird and the turtle looked like they wanted to tell me to just give up. A mouse scrambled up my table, saw me, and ran away, eyes wide. As if she thought I was the killer.

None of these judgey animals were good for me right now. Not one bit.

So, I set Beth's alarm on her shop and locked the door on my way out. I didn't have a key, but this lock didn't need one. Just for unlocking. When I glanced back inside, all the animals were still looking at me. Man, I was not going back to Beth's shop until this whole thing was settled. Maybe it was the caffeine racing through my blood, or the lack of sleep, but they were making my mood worse.

My car was parked in the alley next to Beth's shop, but as I turned toward it, Beth's sister walked up. Shit. She'd been crying. A lot, by the looks of it. But she'd still managed to put on a tight pair of jeans, a low-cut tank top, and styled her long blonde hair in curls. Maybe I was being mean because she'd broken my friend's heart, but I was having a hard time feeling sorry for her in the least bit.

"Is Beth here?" she asked in a wavering voice.

Okay, don't scream. Don't smack her. Forget every moment you watched Beth take care of this jerk. Forget that

Beth gave up going to university to care for her little sister. Just, be an adult. Answer her nicely.

I took a deep breath and searched for the tiny kernel of empathy inside of me. "No, she left a few minutes ago. Are you okay?" God what a stupid question. What was I supposed to do in a situation like this? What was I supposed to say that wasn't going to tear her down even more? The tongue lashing I wanted to give her was of epic proportions. I swallowed the urge once more though and waited for her response.

"Yes. No." She dabbed at her eyes with a napkin she produced from her pocket. "I don't know. The police just left my place. They're ruling Roger's death due to natural circumstances. There were no signs of foul play at all. They're doing an autopsy, but don't think they'll find anything."

Oh, thank goodness. It hadn't been a murder. My heart fluttered in my chest with relief, or maybe it was just the caffeine. I wanted to jump for joy, but not in front of Tiffany. I might think she was a monster for what she did to her sister, but I wouldn't let her turn me into a monster too. It took everything I had not to let the smile that was in my soul show in my face. "Any idea what he was doing at my house?" I asked.

She frowned. "No, there's no reason for him to be anywhere near you, or any of Beth's friends. We were blissfully happy together. He said he didn't miss a thing about having that old, useless--" She saw the thunderous expression on my face, and quickly switched gears. "The thing is, I think there's more going on here than just something natural. That's why I was coming here. I need Beth to help me investigate Roger's death."

"Oh," I whispered. "She should be back soon."

Tiffany nodded. "Thanks."

We stared at each other awkwardly, and I tried to think of a graceful way to end the conversation. As relieved as I was that I might not be on the hook for murder, I did *not* want to help Tiffany. I wanted as far away from this situation as I could get. Not just because of the murder, but because Roger dying didn't erase what Tiffany had done. Nothing could ever erase that.

She drew herself up taller as though she was mentally dusting herself off. "The thing is, I wasn't even sure if I was going to ask her... I've been standing here for a while trying to figure out what to do. But maybe I don't have to. I've heard around town that you've helped Beth with some of her jobs. Do you think you could help me?" Tiffany looked like a con artist who had just found her new target... or maybe I just didn't like her. "It will be so awkward asking Beth, given her history with Roger."

That much was true. It would be awkward for Beth. But Beth was my best friend, and I was more like a ride-or-die type of bitch. No way I'd do something behind Beth's back. "I don't know, Tiffany. I don't feel comfortable not including Beth, however awkward it might be. This is her business above everything else."

"Please," she got that whimpery voice that used to make Beth cave and give her whatever she wanted.

"I don't think so," I said, a little more forcefully.

She pulled her shoulders back. "I know she probably told her side of the story about what happened with Roger. But I just want you to know that he and I found true love with each other. The kind of love that only comes across once in a lifetime. I did Beth a favor by taking him. I mean, would she really want to stay with a guy who wanted to be with me?"

I crossed my arms over my chest, glaring at her. "My husband cheated too. What story do you think his new lady tells people? Probably something like the steaming pile of garbage that you just spewed to try to rewrite why you did one of the worst things imaginable to a woman who loved and raised you? Right?"

Her eyes filled with tears. "Don't be mean to me! My husband just died!"

I couldn't help but roll my eyes and fold my arms over my chest. "Karma's a bitch, sometimes."

She glared back at me and wiped a tear angrily from her cheek, then spun around to march off. But she only made it like two steps, and then her shoulders curved down. Very slowly, she turned back around, and her expression was certainly humbled. Not that I trusted her as far as I could throw her.

"There's something else. I'm afraid Beth might be in danger," she whispered.

Now my suspicion was up. "Why didn't you lead with that?"

Tiffany shrugged. "I don't know. I'm just reeling. I can't think straight."

She looked so pitiful I almost reached out to pull her into my arms, but then stopped myself. "I am sorry he died." Cheaters deserved to be walked through the streets while people pelted them with old, moldy, rotten fruit. They deserved to constantly be able to smell something off in the fridge but never be able to find it, to have an itch they could never scratch, or to never be able to get an ice-cold drink on a hot day. Or even to never be able to taste anything but cabbage for the rest of their life, no matter what they ate. But they didn't deserve to be murdered. At least not in my world.

"So why do you think Beth might be in danger?"

She moved closer to me, then glanced around the alley as if sincerely afraid. "I think a while ago, possibly, well, Roger might've murdered his business partner," she whispered, the confession rushing out of her mouth. I tried not to react. Wow, this girl knew how to pick them. A cheater and a murderer? "Cliff disappeared, and I think someone found out and killed Roger for it."

Okay, so maybe Roger did deserve to die. He murdered his old partner? Man, I was just glad Beth got away from him. Still, as I stared at the young woman, my little bit of empathy was starting to wither away. She'd willingly stayed with someone even when she suspected he killed someone?

I hadn't wanted to get involved in this before. Her words didn't convince me any more that there was a reason for me to care the least bit about Roger's death. And yet... there was still the matter of Beth and how all of this impacted her.

"What does that have to do with Beth?" I said with a sigh.

"She's still part owner of Roger's company. So, what if the person comes after Beth next?" She looked around nervously again. "Look, here's what I've got so far." Pulling a file folder out of the oversized designer bag that hung from her shoulder, she handed it to me and then covered her mouth. "I know you don't like me. I know you don't like Roger. But as much as I might have hurt my sister, I don't want Roger's actions to get her killed."

"Can you tell me more about Cliff's disappearance and why you think Roger had something to do with it?"

She shook her head and stepped backwards. "I already took a huge risk coming here and giving you that. I'm done now. I need to take care of Roger's funeral. You know now, so it's your job to protect Beth. I did my part." Whirling on her heel, Tiffany took off and disappeared down the alley behind my car.

After everything, this was how she acted? I knew I shouldn't be surprised, I mean, the woman had stolen her sister's husband and baby daddy and acted like she was in the right the whole time. But to know that your sister's life might be in danger and claim that it's taken care of by handing a file folder off to someone? That was cold. My skin broke out in goosebumps as though she'd given me literal chills.

As I stared down at the file folder, I wondered what in the world I'd gotten myself into.

## 6

**Emma**

A LITTLE WHILE LATER, I SAT IN THE KITCHEN OF DEVA'S diner, where there was a tiny table tucked away for friends and family. It wasn't that I was starving, more so that I needed Deva's magical food. I felt like the decision about what to do with Beth and her sister was too much for me to handle. It was as if I'd been handed a bomb, and I had no idea when it was going to go off.

The problem was I didn't want it to go off at all. I was scared that it would explode Beth or explode our relationship. Beth was one of the most important people in my life. I never wanted to do anything that would hurt her or drive a wedge between us. She'd already been through so much. She deserved all the happiness she could get in life and here I was trying to decide whether to bring her a big pile of exploding poop.

Karma needed to get her butt in gear because my friend didn't deserve any of this. I wished for the umpteenth time that I had better control over my powers. I knew it was one of those things where practice made perfect, but sometimes instant gratification was nice too, you know?

"Here you go!" Deva said, grinning as she slid a plate with a cheeseburger and fries in front of me. The roasted meat smell combined with the salty fries made my stomach growl in anticipation of the feast I was about to have.

"Thank you so much," I gushed, looking down at the appetizing banquet in front of me.

"It'll calm you right down," she told me, winking, then reached up to pat her hair. Her short black hair had been swept back from her face; the dark curls pulled tight against her head. She wore all black clothes beneath a white apron. Not her usual chef's coat and stripy pants, which made me smile every time I saw them. Around her neck, there was a big necklace, something I suspected Carol had given her. There was a sweep of glittery silver eye shadow on her eyes and her lips had a red lipstick the same color as her necklace.

"You look nice," I said, picking up the giant burger and wondering how exactly I was going to fit it in my mouth without unhinging my jaw. "Marquis coming by today?"

She blushed. The warlock, and favorite doctor in town, had it bad for Deva. As much as I knew she didn't feel ready to date again after Harry, I also knew she had feelings for Marquis. But as with most things in life, I wasn't going to push. I just had to wait for her to realize it. Something I'd realized a while ago, one of those life lessons, if you will, was that most of the time there was only one person that could control you and your thoughts. You. If Deva wanted to date Marquis, she'd have to talk herself into it, or give herself permission to get over Harry and having been underappreciated and decide to take a chance on someone else. No one else could force her to do that though. It was all her.

"Maybe. I-- I don't know. I just--"

"Either way, you look wonderful."

She smiled. "Thanks. I'm feeling just a little like my old self."

It warmed my heart to hear. Maybe she'd finally officially shut down her ex's sad attempts to get back together and give the doctor even a tiny signal that she might be ready for something new. At this point I think he'd take even the smallest glimmer of hope.

A young server pushed past the little swinging door heading into the kitchen, his eyebrows knit together as though he hated what he was about to say. "Uh, I need help with a customer."

"I'm coming," Deva called as she rushed past me, heading for the dining room.

"Take your time." I choked out the words around the huge bite of cheeseburger, laced with calming magic.

The instant the delicious bacon cheeseburger hit my taste buds, I moaned. Deva never skimped on the good stuff. Her food was always covered in things like multiple kinds of ooey-gooey cheese and crispy, melt-in-your-mouth bacon, not to mention the crunchy, tangy pickles that were hidden by the bun. Even the din of the kitchen, servers calling out numbers, cooks slamming around pans, none of it seemed to filter past the amazing sense of calmness and enjoyment that the incredible food left me feeling. Sometimes I even wondered if it was just her wonderful cooking that made me so happy, not even her magic.

For a while I just ate, completely in heaven. And because no one was looking in my direction, I didn't care how "pretty" I ate. I took massive bites of the burger and stuffed fries in my mouth at the same time. Dunking what my ex would call a handful of fries in her homemade ketchup and managing to fit most of them in my mouth in one go. I was shoveling it in as if I hadn't had a good meal in years, which obviously wasn't the case, but this was Deva's cooking we were talking about. This was something special.

When I finished my burger and reached for more fries, finding the plate mostly empty, I sighed and sat back. The food had hit the spot. I patted my belly as though I was rewarding it for the work it was about to do digesting everything. It was exactly what I'd needed, and now that my belly was full and I'd sat down for a minute, I'd calmed down.

Or maybe it was her magic? I had no idea.

"Okay." Deva sighed and plopped down, her dark eyes focusing on me. "What's going on?"

"Are you sure you can stop?" I asked with a grin. I didn't really want to talk about what had happened even though I knew I needed to. "I'd be happy to sample some dessert or another while you work."

She held up one hand. "Nope, I just got the last table's meal out and we've stopped serving lunch. No meals until we prep for dinner." Reaching out a hand, she smiled as someone put a glass of iced tea in it, the amber liquid and slice of lemon looking more than a little refreshing. "Like magic." She took a sip and stared at me. "Spill."

I paused and gathered my thoughts, sipping on my own iced water to buy some time. The slice of lemon that was floating on top of the ice in my glass gave it a nice tang. "Okay, so you know Beth's sister, Tiffany, right?"

She wrinkled her nose and sipped. "Yeah, dead husband, awkward."

"Right." I took a crumble of french fry and popped it into my mouth, crunching on it before I continued. "So, she cornered me today *after* Beth had already left, but before I could escape to my car. Then, she told me she thinks Roger was..." I looked around the kitchen, what I could see of it, and dropped my voice as I finished what I was saying, "*murdered.*"

Deva's mouth flew open in shock. "No."

"Yes." I reached for a tiny piece of bacon. "She said the police have ruled it natural causes, but she doesn't believe any of it. And she wants me to help her investigate it because..." Another surreptitious look around, another lowering of my voice. "She thinks Beth might be next since Beth is part owner of the business Roger owned."

A few drops of tea sloshed out of the glass when Deva slammed it on the table. "No!"

"Yes!" I sat back and sighed. "What do I *do*?"

Deva shook her head slowly as her eyes blinked. She was thinking, rapidly, and I knew she would have a better read on Beth since she had never left town, unlike me, though for the record it was one of my bigger mistakes. I wouldn't take back having my son, but everything else? It could go take a flying leap.

After a few moments Deva said, "You can't tell Beth."

Relief washed through me as she confirmed what I'd already been leaning toward. Plus, Deva didn't seem to have any sway in her opinion, it was solid as a rock. "Okay, that's what I was thinking. I'm so glad you agree. It would just freak Beth out, and I have no idea if she's in any kind of danger yet."

"Right. Why does Tiffany think Beth is a part of this, or that Roger was even murdered to begin with?" Deva picked up her tea again while I turned and pulled the file folder out of my bag.

"I haven't looked at the file yet. I came straight here when she ambushed me, but she mentioned his dead business partner." I opened the file and pushed my plate out of the way so I could spread out the papers.

Deva scooted her chair around to sit beside me. "Whoa," she whispered.

"Yeah." The file was full of articles about Roger's missing business partner and where he was last seen. I skimmed through them until I came across a page of handwritten notes. "This must be Tiffany's handwriting."

We read through it, and it was a list of how Roger had been acting strangely. Fidgety. And he'd mentioned to her that he thought someone had been following him. "That's it?" Deva asked. "That's all she's going off of?"

I shrugged. "Well, if my partner told me someone was following him and then he turned up dead the next day or a few days later, I'd be pretty freaked, too."

Deva nodded thoughtfully. "Well, we're not regular investigators, are we? Maybe if we go to the place where Roger's business partner was last seen we can pick something up."

"Good thinking." I gulped down my tea and pushed to my feet. "Let's go."

Deva laughed as she looked up at me like I was a crazy person. "I can't go now! I've got a dinner shift to prep. Meet me here at nine, the dinner rush will be over, and I can slip away."

I sighed. She was right, of course, but I was impatient. "Okay, what about Carol?"

Deva pursed her lips. "Let's get her to hang out with Beth. Just in case Tiffany was right about Beth being in danger. I don't want to risk Beth's life just because her sister's a jerk ninety percent of the time."

"Good plan." I bent over and pulled her into a quick hug. "I knew you'd have my back."

With my belly full of amazing food and my nerves calmed by Deva's magic, I headed home. In the back of my mind, a tiny thought whispered that I should still tell Beth, but then I pictured the way she carried everything she'd been through with such grace.

No, she didn't need any of this. I didn't need to use Karma's magic to give someone the karma they deserved. And tonight, Beth deserved to be having fun with her friend. Not worrying that she might be in danger. I'd take this on myself for as long as I could, protecting her in a way that her parents, sibling, and partner had failed to do.

I just hoped I was making the right decision.

## 7

## Emma

I SIGHED AND LEANED BACK, BURYING MY TOES UNDER HENRY'S thigh. "This is the life," I mused as Ginger and Fred danced across the TV screen.

This was how Henry and I spent many a night growing up, watching old movies, and eating terrible food. One of the hard things about having an autistic brother was that he wasn't big on affection, or compliments, and sometimes his directness could hurt my feelings. But one of the wonderful things about having an autistic brother was that, when we could share a passion, like movies, it was incredible. He knew so much about everything we watched and noticed things in the films that escaped me. As a kid, I was so excited to watch movies with him, because he was nearly as exciting as the movie itself.

I'd missed it more than I realized. I'd missed *him* more than I realized.

Over the years we'd grown apart, and some of it was Rick's fault, but a lot of it was just because I wasn't there.

Relationships can only stand so much silence and between Rick, having a child, and building our business, the silence had stretched awfully thin between us. Now the silence was gone, and we were rebuilding though. It made me almost grateful for everything that happened.

Henry gave a small smile, his gaze on the screen. "This was nominated for the best foreign film in 1986."

I smiled. "I can see why." The way Fred and Ginger were looking at each other as they twirled across the floor, her dress flying around her, the feathers that adorned it making it look like she was flying, reminded me of something that I wanted to ask. "How are you and Alice?"

Something shifted in his expression, though I couldn't say what, showing me how happy he was when he thought of his girlfriend. "Good. We're playing video games after our movie time. Our online tribe has a plan to finally take on this castle that we haven't been able to beat."

Man, Alice and Henry were seriously perfect for each other. I might not completely understand their relationship, but it worked for them, and it made them happy. That was all that really mattered.

"And does Alice ever want to move in here? What does she think about kids?"

His gaze never left the screen. "She likes her house. Her parents do her laundry and cook. She says kids are fine. Messy and loud. But fine."

That wasn't really what I meant, but it sort of answered my question. I didn't need to be an aunt, as long as they were happy. Some people never had or wanted kids, and that was totally okay. Honestly, waiting and not jumping into things right away might have saved me a lot of heartache, not that I'd ever change having Travis, but I could understand the hesitation.

"And have you been staying away from gambling?" My gut twisted as I asked the question and I forced myself not to hold my breath as I waited for his answer.

His gaze finally left the screen, and a flash of guilt came and went from his face in an instant. "I only gamble online now, not with anyone in town."

Well, at least he wouldn't tick off the shifters or run into the sirens again. I hoped.

The movie kept playing, and I glanced out the big picture window, watching the waves roll over the white sand beaches. Had I really left this place for a guy? Mystic Hollow was idyllic in some ways. From the beaches to the cute little local businesses, to the bed and breakfasts that dotted the outskirts of town. Add in my family and friends living here and how friendly everyone was, except for some grumpy shifters, and I was surprised that this place wasn't overrun by tourists. I wondered if there was some magic at play there, keeping them from staying too long or coming too close.

I knew that technically when I left it had been for college, but I'd always imagined coming back until I met Rick. What was it about love that made people stupid? I supposed there were stupider things I could have done for love, but still.

Despite my best intentions, my thoughts went to Daniel. Would I be crazy to fall for the big shifter? Right now, probably, but for some reason, I felt like I wouldn't have to give up important parts of myself to keep him happy like I had with Rick. I wouldn't need to change myself.

It hadn't happened all at once, it wasn't like I met Rick and he told me I had to do x, y, and z if I wanted us to be together. No, it was the slow nudging to lose weight, to keep dyeing my hair a certain color because that's how he liked it, to get back in shape after having a baby so that he would still find me attractive, not to mention cooking and cleaning everything on my own, raising said baby without his help and still being expected to help run a business and look a certain way. It was exhausting and insidious. It wore me down like water creating the Grand Canyon. I suddenly realized just how controlling he'd been. I knew the next time I found someone I wanted to be in a relationship with they would have to accept me as I came, with no changes, because that wasn't going to fly anymore.

"What are you thinking about?"

I turned and found Henry watching me. "I don't know. I guess how much I really missed this place. How much I gave up for Rick."

His gaze returned to the screen. "I never liked Rick, but he made you happy, so I let it go."

Turning on my side, I snuggled in the blanket and focused on the movie. I want to say I was completely enraptured by the film and that my eyes didn't close but that might have been a lie because halfway through, Henry tapped my leg. "Is that your phone?"

I sat up and pulled my cell from my back pocket. I hadn't even heard it because it was buried under the big blanket. It wasn't because I had been drifting off to sleep. "Oh, it's Travis!" I was excited to hear from my son. He didn't call often enough. "Hey, Pumpkin, how are you?"

"I'm good! I just came home to do laundry. It was kind of weird how quiet the house was."

"Ah, are you missing mama?"

He scoffs. "Nah, I love you, but I don't mind just being able to focus on my friends and school."

"How is all that going?"

"School? Well, I'm doing well in my classes. Just finished

a big test, and I feel like it went well. Super ready to graduate. Friends? Well, I didn't tell you this because I thought you were dealing with enough, but Becca and I broke up. A while ago."

My heart froze in my chest. I thought they would be together for much longer than that. She'd been one of the sweetest girls Travis had ever brought home. "Why didn't you tell me?" My hand had gone to my chest, clutching at my shirt, which was ridiculous. My son was still young enough to be playing the field. Did people still say that? Anyway, he didn't need to bind himself to someone like I'd done with Rick.

"I didn't want to upset you. I mean you just disappeared back to Mystic Hollow, so I wasn't sure what was going on, but I figured you had enough on your plate." He was starting to sound defensive, so I knew I had to rein it back in unless I wanted a grumpy Travis on my hands, and with how rarely he called, that was the last thing I wanted.

"That makes sense, but you can always call me and tell me anything, Pumpkin. You know that, right?" I asked, wanting to make sure he wasn't holding other stuff back because he thought I was too fragile.

"Well, if that's the case then I sort of started seeing someone else..."

I perk up. "Seeing *someone else*?"

"Oh, mom, it's not serious or anything."

But it had to be serious if he was even mentioning her. He never mentioned girls. The only other girl he'd ever seriously talked to me about was Becca, and apparently that was done and dusted now.

"Tell me about her."

He hesitated, and I heard him starting the washer. I swear that boy only ever called me when he did laundry.

"Her name is Jacqueline. She's in the engineering program with me. She's kind of... different."

"Different in a good way?"

I can almost hear him blushing. "Yeah. She has this laugh. Like, when she laughs, I can't help but smile. And she wears sparkly headbands and sings when she walks and... well, she's just fun to be around."

"So, are you dating or just hanging out?" I hold my breath. He'd always kind of been the friend to girls. I remember in high school he always felt like the jerks got the girls that he really liked, but he just wanted them to be happy.

Sure, he'd brought a couple girls over and said they were his girlfriends, but it was only ever once or twice, and they usually stopped hanging out quickly after that. I always thought it was just because he was so smart and kind. Girls that age weren't always ready for someone like Travis.

He told me he wasn't sure what they were yet, but I could tell from his tone that he wanted it to be more than just hanging out. I hoped my baby didn't get his heart broken. If he did though, he was a big boy and could handle himself. I had loved the idea of him moving to Mystic Hollow though and I made a mental note to ask him about that the next time we spoke. Although I would probably forget unless I wrote it down.

When we hung up, I filled Henry in on his nephew's life before we settled back in to finish the movie. "Remember when we were kids, we'd do our hair all crazy and put our underwear on our heads and have a pajama day?"

He chuckled. "Yeah. That was a long time ago." His gaze drifted back to the movie, not giving me nearly enough reminiscing about the underwear-head thing. "Be right back," I muttered.

I ran down the hall and grabbed my granniest pair of panties, put them on my head, then pulled my hair out through the leg holes to stick up like crazy.

As I ran back down the hall, I sang an old song we used to drive each other nuts with. "This is the song that doesn't —" I stopped short when I jumped off the stairs and saw Henry standing with someone in the foyer.

"Hey," Daniel said lamely.

I yanked the underwear off my head as I squeaked out some sort of greeting. "I didn't know you were coming by."

"Yeah, I wanted to check on you after what happened." He looked like he was fighting hard not to burst out laughing.

"I'm good. Just hanging out here with Henry, watching a movie." Belatedly, I realized I was talking with my hands and swinging the underwear around at the same time. I stepped back and stuffed them into my back pocket.

"Can we talk?" Daniel asked with a big grin on his face. He nodded at Henry. "In private."

## 8

## Emma

Opening the back door, Daniel waited for me to go out then shut the door behind us with a quiet snick. "Please," I motioned toward the glider. It was a two-seater, that matched the two Adirondack chairs that sat out there as well. I knew men often liked to spread out, so I figured that was the best option for him. "Sit."

He did, and then patted the spot beside him. I perched on the edge, barely letting my whole ass fit on the chair, not wanting to crowd him, as nerves fluttered in my belly. It had to be because I didn't know what he was going to say, right? He looked so relaxed sitting there though, like he would be at ease anywhere. It made me almost want to lean back into him and absorb some of the chill attitude he had. And maybe enjoy watching the waves with the arm of a handsome man around my shoulders. So, sue me.

"I came to tell you that you're no longer considered a suspect." He grinned at me as I looked over at him. His eyes sparkled in the low light. "In my official capacity as retired sheriff, I got the skinny."

I patted his knee, surprising myself or maybe even both of us with the contact and smiled. "Thank you, but I already knew. Beth's sister told me." I hesitated and looked out at the waves with my hand still on Daniel's knee. I knew I should remove it, that to leave it there might be considered inappropriate, but I couldn't bring myself to let go. When he put his hand over mine, I decided to trust him. "There's something else, though. I don't think it was a natural death, no matter what the police have ruled it as."

He sat back, accidentally dislodging my hand, but he caught it and twined our fingers together. My heart swelled with the small sign of affection. He had enjoyed having my hand on his knee. In fact, he enjoyed it so much that he didn't want to let my hand go, which was why it was now wrapped in his much larger one. His voice was careful, quiet, like he didn't want to scare me off, as though I was some wild creature needing to be approached with caution, as he asked, "Why do you think that?"

"So, Roger had a partner. He disappeared five years ago. Do you remember that?" I hoped that Daniel might have information he would share with me about what happened, or at least what they think happened.

Daniel sighed, frustration and disappointment warring in his gaze. "I was on the force when that guy disappeared. I couldn't find anything." He squeezed my hand. "That case always bothered me."

"Do you have any information at all?" I asked. I hadn't yet told him I was thinking of investigating this on my own. I wasn't sure how he'd react. I wasn't sure how anyone would react, or at least anyone who knew me and my new skill set. It wasn't as though I was Veronica Mars or something and adding karma into the mix just made everything more complicated.

"Not really. If you thought Roger was an ass, you should've met Cliff. He was a real dick." He ducked his head and seemed to mentally scold himself. "Pardon the language."

I snorted and squeezed his hand. Worrying about language in front of me was adorable, but I wasn't a little girl. I'd heard worse and had much worse directed at me personally and from my husband as well, or at least he had been at the time. Not that I wanted to think about Rick right now. He always had a way of ruining the moment. "Don't worry on my account. What else?"

"He was hated by pretty much everyone in town, so the list of suspects was substantial. But nobody panned out."

I wavered, but I had to give him more information in order to *get* more information from him. "I think Beth might be in trouble. I think someone went after her ex, and since she's still part-owner of the business, I'm scared they'll go after Beth. I don't know what I'd do if anything happened to her."

He furrowed his brow. "I don't think she's in any danger," he said. "Unless Roger had something to do with Cliff's disappearance, or if Beth had something to do with it, why would anyone go after either of them?"

His words sounded good, but his eyes looked worried. The reassuring smile he gave me didn't quite touch those mossy green orbs, and I knew there was something about the case he wasn't telling me, something that would make him worry about Beth too now that I'd planted that seed.

I wanted to tell him everything, to bare my soul to those observant green eyes of his, but I couldn't. Not yet anyway. I needed to know what happened to Cliff before I told him anything else. I didn't want to accidentally implicate Beth just because I didn't understand something or didn't have all of the information. I knew everything supernatural in Mystic Hollow was new to me, so I wanted to be extra careful, especially when it came to my friends.

An awkward silence stretched between us, so I turned my gaze toward the ocean in the distance. The quiet rush of the waves hitting the shore filled the air along with a few bird calls. The white foam of the waves washed up the beach as though it was desperately trying to escape the rest of the ocean, only to fail and be reclaimed by it once again. In some ways, it felt like Mystic Hollow was reclaiming me. I took a risk and glanced at Daniel again only to find him watching me. I turned my head back to face the white caps. It was safer that way. No tempting gazes trying to make me spill my guts.

"So," Daniel said, sounding just as awkward as I felt. "How do you like being back in town?"

"I'm pretty happy," I admitted. "I don't want to go back." I paused, considering his question properly before I answered any further. The idea of living with Henry was strange, homey but strange. There weren't many middle-aged women that lived with their equally middle-aged brothers. I wasn't ashamed about it, far from it, but if I was to theoretically start dating again at some point there may be some awkward moments in store. Though Daniel seeing me with my undies on my head and Henry acting as though everything was completely normal and something I did every night ranked up there with some of my top awkward moments as an adult. I had to rank adult and teenager awkward moments separately because I was a super awkward teen.

I couldn't help but remember some of the awkward

moments I'd had with Daniel as a teen. I'd had the biggest crush on him then and if I was honest, ever since I'd come back to Mystic Hollow, it had been coming back. How could a woman resist a man like him? Tall, muscular, dark hair, green eyes. He was the definition of dreamy.

After being silent for what was probably too long, I added, "In fact, I'm seriously considering selling my home and staying here with Henry permanently."

His eyebrows flew up as his eyes brightened, making my heart thaw just a little from the block of ice my ex had turned it into. "I vote for that. You being here permanently, I mean."

Standing, Daniel paced a few steps away before turning back to look at me. "Have you tried the new sushi restaurant in town?"

I shook my head. "No, not yet."

He scuffed his toe on the deck. It was almost like time had flashed backward and I could see the high school version of him that I'd always dreamed would ask me out one day. "It's good."

"I do like sushi," I said, hoping he was leading up to what I suspected he was. I was more than ready for him to ask me out on a date. I wasn't about to jump into a serious relationship, my heart was still healing from my last one, but I could handle a date, especially with a man like Daniel. Maybe I should take the plunge and suggest it myself. Standing, I walked over to him. "I need to try that sushi place," I hinted strongly.

Daniel looked over my shoulder into the house. Stepping back to the glider, he picked up my God-awful granny panties and handed them to me. "I'll, uh, talk to you soon, okay?"

Son of a... I shoved them back in my pocket, deeper this

time. "Sure," I said in a voice that was far too bright. "I'll walk you out."

Again, with the awkward silence. I followed him to the front door. His butt looked great in those jeans, just the thought had me yanking my gaze upward and fixing it on the point between his shoulder blades. "Thanks for stopping by to tell me about the lack of murder charges," I said in a quiet voice as he reached for the handle on the front door.

Daniel nodded. "Sure, sure."

He stepped outside, and when I shut the door, I ran to the living room to look out of the window and got there just in time to see him slap himself in the forehead. His mouth moved and I had to assume he was berating himself, just like I had been doing to myself mentally. Part of me wished I could hear what he was saying, but mainly I was just glad that at least he was as embarrassed as I was.

## 9

## Emma

I WAITED AT THE LITTLE TABLE IN THE CORNER OF THE KITCHEN again while Deva gave her kitchen crew last-minute instructions. She was too much of a micromanager, but it meant I got to eat those amazing truffle oil fries she'd served with dinner along with the leftover très leches shortcake pieces they had offered as dessert while I waited, so whatever. I wasn't about to turn down food like that.

"Did you put confidence in this?" I whispered as she hurried by, the air gusting behind her and swirling all the delicious scents from the kitchen at me once again. My stomach practically growled as it reignited my hunger. I swear I could eat my talented friend's food every day for the rest of my life and not object. She really was one of the most amazing chefs I'd ever had the privilege of experiencing.

Deva just winked and tapped the side of her nose. A grin tugged at the corners of her mouth, though she didn't bust out a full smile, since she was usually more serious in the kitchen.

Whatever. At least I wasn't scared about doing this investigating thing anymore. We could do this; we were capable women. We were mothers for crying out loud. If we could figure out how to raise crotch goblins into human beings, then we could do anything.

A few minutes later, Deva stopped beside the table, finally standing still for more than thirty seconds. She was wearing real clothes instead of her white—and food-stained—chef's jacket and those strange black and white striped pants that chefs were always wearing. None of it looked very comfortable to me. Okay, the pants weren't so bad since they looked kind of like sweatpants, but the jacket and the way it buttoned around the throat? No thank you. "Let's go."

I pushed to my feet snagging a few last fries and stuffing them into my mouth as I followed her to her car. There wasn't a single nervous butterfly in sight, and my heartbeat was as steady and strong as a drum. "Where are we going?" I asked, figuring I should at least be somewhat mentally prepared for whatever was about to go down.

"The last place Cliff was seen. Roger's law office." Her voice was grim, determined. It made me a little nervous again, so I pulled out the piece of shortbread I'd taken as well and popped it in my mouth, which made Deva smile. She waited patiently for me to finish, laughing softly to herself at my antics with her food.

Once I was done chewing, I took a deep breath and said, "Okay." I hopped in the passenger seat.

Deva yanked a black duffle bag out of the backseat and put it in my lap. The canvas material was rough against my fingertips as I searched for the zipper in the low light. A black zipper on a black bag in a dark car wasn't exactly easy to find. She rattled off the contents as she pulled out of the parking lot of her restaurant. "Flashlights, pepper spray, a letter opener, gloves both nitrile and leather..."

I buckled up and peeked into the bag after finally finding the zipper. "A lockpick?"

She grinned and her eyes flashed with what I swear was excitement. "We gotta get in somehow."

We chatted lightly on the way, mainly trying to keep my mind off the coming danger. It wasn't that I expected something to go wrong, but it just always seemed like it did, so I figured it was better to expect it than to not. I wasn't sure if I was overreacting. For all we knew a guy had just had a heart attack while out for a walk. But when it came to my friends, it was better to be safe than sorry.

Deva's mouth curled into a frown as she glanced in her rearview mirror.

"What's wrong?" I asked, wondering if danger had already found us.

"Just some jerk tailgating us."

"Ugh!" I turned around and saw some giant truck, that was so shiny it'd clearly never hauled a darn thing, so close to the back of Deva's car that I couldn't see his front lights, but his high beams seemed to be turned on. "I hate when people do that. It's not even like we're driving too slow."

Suddenly, the car honked, five quick honks, then he sped into the lane next to us. The lane facing oncoming traffic. Deva gasped, and her hands white-knuckled the steering wheel. Then, he swerved in front of us and stepped on his brakes. Deva squeaked and slammed on her brakes too, which was the only reason we didn't hit the back of his truck.

When he sped back up, Deva and I were both breathing hard. "Sorry," I said, "Car stuff is still pretty triggering for me."

The car accident that killed my parents was a long time ago, and therapy had helped a whole lot to ensure I didn't break out into a cold sweat every time I got into a car, but I still didn't like stuff like this. It brought me back to a dark place that I didn't like.

"That guy was an ass. I'm sorry, Emma. There's always a couple of them, and Bubba likes to drive aggressively. He's caused a few minor accidents over the years."

My teeth clenched together. "A guy like that is going to get someone killed. Unless someone teaches him a lesson." I stretched out my hand toward the truck. "Slow down," I whispered to Deva.

Deva does, giving him a wide berth.

Suddenly, all four of his tires popped, and his car made a terrible sound as it screeched to a halt. He climbed out of his car, in what looked like a fit of rage, but then saw his tires. His mouth dropped open in utter disbelief.

Deva waited for the other side of the road to be clear, then started to go around him. I couldn't help myself. I unrolled my window and yelled, "Karma isn't going to be done with you. Not until you learn how to drive safer."

He looked up at me in confusion, but we just drove past and continued onto the office.

"You're getting more confident," Deva mused, a smile on her lips. "Remember when you popped that spot thief's tires? You were scared. Now, you're a badass."

I grinned. "Or maybe I'm already getting bored with my powers and doing the same things."

She laughed. "Nah, punishing terrible drivers would be near the top of my list if I had your powers."

We were both cackling like old witches but then relaxed again into our drive. But very quickly, my thoughts went back to Daniel. It'd been so dang long since I'd had to date or flirt with anyone. Deva had been single longer, even though she hadn't dated anyone yet. I figured she might be a good person to talk about it all with, but for some weird reason, I felt nervous.

After a few minutes, I glanced at Deva out of the corner of my eye and then decided to just go for it. "So, Daniel tried to ask me out today."

"No!" Deva exclaimed. The grin on her face and lack of true surprise in her voice told me that she thought it was long overdue.

"Yes. But I made a fool of myself and he never got around to asking." At least I was pretty sure he was just being shy and backward like me. Otherwise, he wouldn't have slapped himself in the forehead... would he?

We talked about it all the way to Roger's office, which took a big load off the ride. Deva helped me over-analyze every little detail, down to the type of granny panties I'd had on my head when he first saw me. It made me laugh and relax and almost forget what we were doing. She didn't seem bothered by what we were about to do in the slightest which helped as well, though it made me wonder how common stuff like this was for my friends. How much had I missed out on when I was only a human? It sure seemed like a lot now.

When our conversation died down, I cautiously brought up her dating life. "So, is Harry still trying to get back together with you?"

She stiffened and all her humor died away. "Yeah, I've told him over and over again that I just need space, but I know it's time to have a frank discussion... now that I know how I feel."

"And how do you feel?" I waited, hoping she wasn't seriously considering getting back together with him.

"I feel like I stopped loving him one day at a time. Every time he ignored me. Every time he rejected me. Every time he compared me to other women. It doesn't matter how many flowers he buys or terrible poems he writes now, my love for him is gone."

And yet there was still pain in her voice. "So, you're going to have that conversation with him. And then, are you going to go out with Marquis?"

She was quiet for a minute. "Yeah. I think so, although he's not the reason for my decision. He's more of a bonus. Because I don't know if he's my happily-ever-after, or if I'm too old for all that nonsense."

"You're never too old for a happily-ever-after," I told her.

She gave me a shy smile. "I guess you're right. So, the next time Marquis seems to be hinting for a date, I think I'll take him up on it, and just see where it goes."

"I'm happy for you," I said, and meant it. "I feel like things with Daniel can't really start until everything is completely closed with my ex. It's like you're where I want to be."

She turned on her blinker and slowly turned into a parking lot. "It took me a long time to get to this point. But it's okay if you don't need all that time. No two people have the same path in life."

"You're pretty dang wise."

She grinned. "With age comes wisdom."

"Then, as a person who's a few months older than you, I better get that wisdom faster!"

We were laughing again as we pulled into a parking spot.

"Okay," Deva said as we stared at the small building. The last one on Main Street, a little one-room number. It looked like he hadn't been taking very good care of it if I was honest. The building itself was fine, maybe some paint peeling here and there, but the grass was overgrown and the flower beds that decorated the front and the pathway were full of weeds. I could only imagine the fit my old Homeowners Association would have thrown if I let the house, I had with Rick get to this state. In fact, it probably was in rough shape since I'd abandoned it. I made a mental note to get a landscaping company out there to clean up before I got fined for my grass being too long or something.

As I thought about the town and how different it was from where I lived with Rick, I remembered that for the most part, Roger had been the only lawyer in Mystic Hollow.

Now there were none.

We popped open our car doors and climbed out. I tucked the leather gloves in my back pocket before we crossed the parking lot in a hurry, so we weren't as noticeable. We were each holding the nitrile gloves, and I had a flashlight tucked in my armpit as well as a few of the other accessories Deva had provided. When we approached the small building, music assaulted our ears. "What the hell?" I whispered. "Should we run?"

"There are no cars here," Deva said, looking around. "And the one who might be here, playing music, has just died. My gut says it's tied to whatever is going on with Beth. But I guess the other alternative is that the town teenagers heard he was dead and decided to have some unsupervised fun."

"So... we just march into some kind of dead guy party?"

She shrugged. "If we want answers. And we'll just act like old, confused ladies, who went in the wrong building, if we run into trouble."

I wrinkled my nose. "Are we really old enough to play that card?"

"If they're teenagers," she waves off my comment. "We could be forty or eighty to them. Everyone is just old."

She had a point. So, maybe, the strange party person was connected to this case. Or a bunch of teens we could kick out and get our info. Either way, I hoped we weren't being dumb by not just running the heck out of here

The front door was cracked open. Deva and I donned the nitrile gloves and each of us held a flashlight and a little can of pepper spray. "Remember," she whispered. "If you have to spray it, don't do it in my direction."

I nodded. "Let's go."

We walked in as slowly and quietly as we could. The small front hallway was empty with all the music coming from a room in the back.

Switching on our flashlights, the beams of light bouncing off the dark walls, we hurried toward the source of the noise, then threw the door open and shined our flashlights in.

A dozen or so ghosts froze mid-dance and stared at us in horror. The music kept bumping away but none of them so much as twitched as though Deva and I were T-Rexes and could sense movement. My gaze traveled over the crowd of ghosts. Each of them was a shade of gray, ranging from almost black to almost white, but never quite reaching either, and glowing ever so slightly just like the ghost on my porch. They all drifted a foot or so off the ground and their bodies faded in a way where it wasn't clear if they had feet or not.

Deva sighed as they disappeared one by one. They didn't pop out of existence all at once like a blink and they were gone kind of thing, it was more like when you looked at a bright light and looked away you could still see it in a way, but eventually it faded. A couple of them hung around giving us grumpy looks. "Come on, guys," she said. "If you let us ask a few questions we'll leave you to it."

I looked at my friend in surprise. Could we just casually chat with ghosts? I had no idea how any of this stuff worked, but it seemed strange.

My mouth opened to ask Deva exactly that when one older man rolled his eyes but floated over. His form seemed to bob like a duck on the surface of a lake as the waves moved it along, or like he was walking on the moon, like gravity just didn't really affect him anymore. If I hadn't already become Karma, had witches as friends, reversed a siren curse, and scolded shifters, I'd be freaked out.

Okay, so I was still a little freaked out.

He glanced at me, as if he knew how uncertain I felt, before looking back to Deva. "What is it?"

"We're investigating Roger's death, and his partner, Cliff, who is still missing." Deva's words were calm and measured as though she was trying not to scare him.

He squinted his eyes at us. "You should really just let this go."

Oh, that wasn't suspicious. Not at all.

"Listen, if we don't figure it out, Beth could be in danger," I said, jumping in before he could fade away as well.

The ghost snapped his gaze back to me and sighed. "Okay. I do like Beth. She was always so nice to us. And never worried about us partying here when they were closed." He sort of hissed and faded a bit. "It's a shame, really."

"What's a shame?" Deva asked. "What do you mean?"

Worry coursed through my chest making my heart beat

a staccato rhythm and my breath freeze in my lungs as I waited for his answer.

The ghost faded a bit more. "Whatever killed Roger will definitely come for Beth."

Then he disappeared.

"Shit," Deva hissed. "We have to go."

I nodded, when someone suddenly screamed "Boo!" behind me.

Shrieking, I dove away from the person and went flying over a spinning office chair on my back. For one brief moment, the air was knocked out of me, and I was like a turtle on my back, lying unable to move, and then I sucked in a deep breath. Breathing hard, I scrambled to sit up, even though my back was killing me, then glanced at a young ghost who was already starting to fade again.

"That was mean, Oliver!" Deva shouted, shaking her fist at him.

The ghost, who was apparently named Oliver, pouted. "No one ever lets me have any fun!"

"Fun?" I screamed the word, climbing to my feet. I grabbed for my pepper spray and ran toward him.

"Don't!" Deva shouted.

I sprayed.

The air instantly became thick, and the peppery taste of the spray seemed to surround me. Deva and I both started coughing and ran for the door, but I could hear the sound of dozens of ghosts laughing behind us. When we got outside, we both continued to cough for a while.

At last, Deva looked at me, wiping her eyes. "Pepper spray doesn't work on ghosts."

"I realize that was a dumb move, okay? At the time, I just wanted to teach the little shit a lesson."

"Well, you taught him one," she said, smirking.

We found a water fountain and washed out our eyes. Then, with our faces half in our shirts, we went back into the office but found it empty. Deva switched off the music, cursed all the ghosts, and we headed back out.

Well, I felt like an idiot. But more than that, I was scared. The ghost had said Beth was in danger. And given the look on Deva's face, I suspected that she trusted what he'd said.

Now, we definitely had a case.

## 10

**Carol**

"What a bitch," I muttered as my knitting needles clacked in front of me. "They should vote her off."

Beth giggled. "They don't vote the real housewives off the show."

I shrugged and grabbed my glass of wine. "They should, I bet it would make it more interesting if they had to compete to stay on."

"I don't think I could handle the backstabbing being any worse than it already is. The drama would just be too much," Beth said, shaking her head as she mimicked me and took a sip of her own wine.

We'd had a few glasses each and I could tell we were both feeling it. Beth's cheeks had flushed, and she was laughing at things that weren't really that funny. I didn't mind though, as long as she was having a good time. When Deva and Emma told me what was going on, I wasn't sure that keeping it from Beth was the right thing to do. I thought she had a right to know she was in danger, but they'd convinced me she would be better off not knowing and now here we were.

I'd convinced her to come spend the evening with me at my house. Well, technically, it was now Deva's and my house. When she first moved in, it kind of felt like she was a guest, unsure of her marriage or her future. Now, I couldn't imagine the house without her. Having Beth here for the evening too only added to how much I loved my little cottage. I just felt comfortable here, around my own stuff. My yarn wall was bright and colorful, making me cheerful every time I looked at it. Plus, I could just imagine all the projects I'd be able to do with the yarn which always got me excited and my brain buzzing.

The opposite wall had my mural on it, a cherry blossom tree started in the corner and the branches spread over the entire wall sheltering the peacocks that were painted underneath. Their names were Blanche and Gulliver, and they were in a very devoted relationship with each other. Deva had insisted on moving the TV to the plain wall because she said she couldn't concentrate on it when the wall behind it was so busy. Apparently, my fluffy cushions and disco ball were unusual decorations as well, I just thought they were fun. They made me feel sparkly and happy.

Deva had the place organized to the nth degree, but at least it had my flair. All my house plants were hanging or on windowsills, some even got pride of place on the coffee table. What can I say? I like having something to take care of and plants don't exactly demand much, neither did cats for that matter. The plants' leaves were all regularly dusted now, and she'd picked me up some of those automatic watering things that look like little glass balls that you stick in the pot so, even if I forgot, they weren't going to die.

She had also picked up all the loose balls of yarn that

had been all over the place and stacked them next to the yarn wall so I could find them more easily. It was very thoughtful, but I kind of liked the odd ball of brightly colored yarn here and there. Plus, my cats played with them, so it was a constant battle between Deva picking the yarn up and the cats dragging them all over the place. I let them have at it though because I knew my tastes weren't the same as everyone else's. I couldn't predict who was going to come out on top, the cats or Deva. It varied every day.

My gaze flicked back to the television and I realized that all the blonde, tan women were starting to merge into one in my mind. Their perfectly coiffed hair, blemish-free skin, and bright white teeth were all a little overwhelming. Did real people look like that?

I drained my glass as I contemplated how realistic it was that those women all looked like that naturally. Unlikely, I decided. Probably years of surgery, strict workout routines, and horrible diets. I guessed I could look like them if I really wanted to.

And then, my stomach growled. I patted my soft belly, silently reassuring it that I'd never do that to us and thought about what I could start shoveling. Deva had sent over some brownies she'd made just for Beth. They had some sort of protection charm on them. And a brownie sounded good.

"Refill?"

Beth didn't look away from the screen. "Yeah. And are those *real*? Isn't she like our age? Why aren't her boobs hanging in that dress?"

I laughed. "Nothing about that woman is real, trust me."

"I don't think there's enough tape in the world that could keep my boobs up that high and not swinging out of a dress like that. Heck, I think they'd be flapping around in the wind on a boat, looking like stretchy arms."

Oh my gosh, I could freaking picture us all on that boat. One of us would have our skirt over our head. Another one would have boobs flopping out. And I'd be the one burnt to a crisp with my hair so tangled that people would scream when I got back to land.

Man, they should make a show about us. Real Middle-Aged Women, Caution: Horrifyingly Realistic Women Up Ahead. There would be whole episodes about us diving into pre-menopause. Viewers would find themselves losing their appetites and wondering why it'd been so long since I last shaved. They'd watch us eat and be inspired not to look like us one day. Yeah, right. Like old age wasn't coming for every-one, one day.

I started laughing, and Beth finally looked in my direction.

"What?"

"Just thinking about us on a boat."

"We can rent a boat, but I'm not shaving," she muttered.

"Me neither! We'd end up on some Big Foot sighting websites!"

She grinned.

I reached for my glass, then remembered it was empty. Stupid wine. There was never enough when I wanted it. And the kitchen seemed *so* far. But no, I was here for Beth. If we were out of wine, I'd be the hero who brought us more!

Empty glasses in hand I popped up from my seat, or tried to, my knee locked up slightly and I had to bend it again to loosen it up and headed into the kitchen to refill our glasses and get us each another brownie.

Sure, Beth hadn't asked for one, but her glass was empty just like mine and if I was getting another brownie then the polite thing was to bring her one as well. Plus, she was much more engrossed in the show than I was. I preferred those baking shows where everyone was super nice and helpful to one another. Their accents were adorable as well, so that didn't hurt matters.

Something or someone tapped on our kitchen window as I poured more wine for Beth. I froze. What the hell was that?

Peering outside, I didn't see anything. Just my old familiar tree. Still, I kept staring for a long minute, not feeling comfortable until I noticed leaves dancing along the grass in the glow from the backlight. Dancing. Sigh. In the wind, of course.

I blamed my nervous reaction on my tipsy state. It was probably just a branch being knocked against the window by the wind. I bit into one of the brownies before I filled up my glass with wine as well. One thing I'd learned about living alone for most of my life is that I couldn't jump at every tiny sound, or I'd go insane.

I hadn't thought things through though, and when I tried to carry the brownies and the two glasses of wine back, I nearly spilled. Losing the wine and the brownies would have been a tragedy.

As I moved to return to the living room, with the brownies precariously balanced on top of the wine glasses, someone tapped on the back door. I startled and my brownie fell into my glass, the missing bite making it more unstable than Beth's. I cursed under my breath and turned back to the kitchen, setting everything down on the counter. Chocolate and red wine went together, right? Surely, I didn't just ruin both.

Okay, now. Somebody had to be teasing me. Maybe Deva and Emma had finished investigating and were back to freak us out. They should know better, but I also remembered how mischievous they'd been when we were all younger. I yanked open the back door. "Gotcha!" I yelled.

But nobody was there.

With a sigh, I stuck my head outside and looked around. The trash cans were where I'd left them, the flowers were swaying in the night breeze, but there was no explanation for the tapping noise I'd heard.

Nobody.

"Weird," I murmured to myself as a chill broke out over my skin.

I turned back inside, pulling the door closed with me, and shrieked when I found a man standing behind me, holding a knife up in the air. My knife if the pearlescent handle was anything to go by. Seemed like a silly thing to notice but I loved my knife set. A black hood covered his head, hanging down over his face shadowing it, but even so, I could tell that he was wearing something under it as well, some kind of mask that made him look animalistic. He roared at me and lunged, striking outward and making me scream once more. Fear clenched around my heart as my mind went blank of any spell I could use.

One of my cats jumped off the table that sat between the living room and the kitchen and onto his back, sinking her claws deep into his skin. The man screamed and dropped my kitchen knife as he lurched forward. I stepped to the side and grabbed my kitty around the waist, yanking her back toward me as the man bolted out the back door, swinging it open with such force that it bounced backward and smacked him in the face before he could actually get away.

Kitty's claws came back with a bit of the guy's back, so he screamed louder as he finally made it out of the house.

Beth came running in, also screaming, or maybe it was supposed to be a war cry with the way she was brandishing the TV remote. I wasn't sure. This kind of thing demanded action though, so I put my kitty down and yanked open the kitchen drawer that held emergency hex bags for just such a time as this. "Come on!" I yelled.

We ran out the back door, going as fast as we could, around the house and up the street. We were a ways back, not a chance of being as fast as our attacker, but we saw him cross the road and disappear into the woods. I started to follow, but Beth jerked me back just in time to keep from getting hit by a car. It hadn't been going that fast, but the tires squealed against the tarmac nonetheless as it ground to a halt in front of us.

I would've gone around it and kept running after him, but Emma popped out of the passenger seat of the car, which I now recognized as Deva's. "What's going on?" Emma demanded, looking ready to set the whole world alight if she needed to.

Dejected, I glared toward the spot where the man disappeared. "Trouble."

## 11

**Emma**

"Well, now what?" Deva shook her head and settled deeper into the sofa. The thing was ridiculously comfortable, to the point that I wondered if my friends had somehow used their magic to make it that way. The paisley fabric screamed Carol's tastes and I wasn't surprised that half of it was covered in a blanket, and I'd bet money this was where Deva sat regularly. Unfortunately, that was the space that Beth was currently occupying, so Deva was sitting next to her, while Carol and I sat on... bean bags? I wasn't sure where they had appeared from, but one of them was covered in cat hair. Not that I really minded, but it was clear that I was stealing a cat's bed and I didn't want any more cats to be angry with me.

"I think we all agree Roger was murdered," Beth said in a wooden voice, her gaze fixed on a potted plant that sat on the coffee table between us. "But what I don't understand is why they'd come after me. And why, after Roger's death has been ruled natural, the man would come in, attack us with a knife and try to kill us in a decidedly *un*natural way?"

"Could it be something to do with the company itself?" I asked. I knew Rick would fight me tooth and nail to maintain control of the company if he wanted it in the divorce. It wasn't like I was the one who'd built it from the ground up or anything, no, I was just the wife. Right.

Beth shrugged. "We did a lot of bankruptcies, divorces, prenups, property disputes, that kind of thing. Usually fairly amicable stuff though some of the divorces and property disputes got nasty. No one ever blamed us for it though. It wasn't like Roger was a defense attorney, getting felons off their charges. Who would we have pissed off?"

"Daniel made it sound like no one liked Cliff, but he didn't really have anything to say about Roger. Could it be a client that was Cliff's but took it out on Roger instead?" I asked.

Beth shot me what was almost a glare. She hadn't been happy when we told her about everything, and that was one of the biggest understatements of the year. She huffed and said, "Maybe. Cliff was a lot... riskier with his clientele than Roger was. It was one of the things that drove them apart. Roger wanted to stick with more small-town stuff whereas Cliff wanted to make a name for himself, attract top-dollar clients. I don't think that whoever Cliff pissed off would hurt me though. That seems unnecessary when the two men they would have interacted with are both dead or missing."

"What about an inheritance?" Deva asked, glancing at Beth warily. Neither of us were in our friend's good graces right now.

Beth shrugged. "It's not *that* much. And it'll just go to my girls when I die, so unless this person is ready to kill us all, it's not worth all this. The main part of the business is probably the building if I'm being honest. I just hope that if something did happen to me as well, the ghosts wouldn't be complete jerks and would let my girls sell it before they started up their nightly raves again."

My blood ran cold at the thought that someone might try to kill Beth's kids, too. That couldn't happen. I didn't care what we had to do, but our kids were staying well out of it.

Deva rustled through the papers that Beth's lawyer had sent over. The man must have had nothing better to do tonight because though we didn't expect them till the morning, a special courier had dropped them off an hour ago. "Maybe it has nothing to do with his partner. Just your ex." She shrugged and kept reading. "I'm not seeing anything significant here."

"Could it be an old client?" I asked. "I mean I know you said that Roger didn't take any cases where things got particularly nasty, but that doesn't mean that people just let stuff go. Some hold grudges. Maybe it was a client that the two of them worked with together or something?"

Deva made a noise low in her throat. "Could be, considering the partner went missing *exactly* five years from the day Roger was murdered. That can't be insignificant."

"Why would it be?" I asked. Yes, it was odd, but it couldn't mean that much could it? Then again, I was new to all this stuff. Looking at the expressions my friends were wearing made me feel like a naive child. There was a reason, a magical one, which means one I wouldn't have thought of before karma came into my life and shook everything up.

Carol sighed. "Unfortunately, an anniversary gives a witch a significant event to siphon energy and power from. It's a conduit of sorts. Think of it like a straw in a drink. Sure, you can drink it normally, but if you're sucking on the liquid with a straw then it makes it easier to get it into your mouth and consume it."

That's it. I'm making a damn handbook. Every time I think I've got a handle on something it up and gets more complicated. The only problem was that I knew I'd never remember to write everything down. One of these days though, I was going to understand all this supernatural stuff and then everyone would be in trouble. Karma would know exactly what she was doing, which would make a nice change.

"I guess we need to go talk to the witches," Carol said. "That's got to be our next move."

Each of them looked as upset as the other. Carol seemed to suddenly need to knit, while Deva looked like she was trying to set the peacock that was painted on the wall on fire with just her gaze and Beth... she still had that same angry but distracted expression on her face.

"What?" I asked, again feeling like the ignorant outsider. I hadn't even known there were witches or anything supernatural in town when I was growing up and now? Now, I knew they were there, but I had no idea who was what. I mean was the postman a shifter? Was the cashier at the grocery store a witch? Anyone could be anything, it was truly mind-blowing. The only creatures I'd met that might stand out were vampires and sirens, mainly because of their skin tones and the fact that they seemed to have a unique way of moving through the world.

"It just bothers us to think it could be one of our own," Deva whispered. "Using magic to murder isn't natural. It means the witch has gone dark."

They all shook their heads. If I had walked in at that moment, I would have asked who died. That was how serious and sad they all looked. They didn't even know who it was that might have turned to the dark side, but they were acting like it was one of their friends that had betrayed them and everything that witches stood for by committing murder using magic.

I knew the murderer wasn't in the room with us, but clearly, the three of them had complicated feelings when it came to the other witches in the community. They hardly ever talked about them and I hadn't been introduced to anyone, so it was like they didn't want anything to do with them. Yet, their reaction to one of them using dark magic was the opposite, like they were best friends with all of them.

I had to assume it was more of a community loss since I didn't want to ask yet another question when they all looked like someone had just kicked them when they were down. The last thing I wanted to do was add to the stress and disappointment they were feeling by picking apart their feelings on what was happening.

What were we going to find now?

## 12

## Daniel

I LET THE AXE FLY, SWINGING DOWNWARD WITH A SLIGHT whistle through the air as I carefully steered it in the right direction, and split the wood cleanly. The log cracked apart, splinters flying, as the ax split it. I pulled the pieces up one at a time and did it again until they were the right size.

The scent of fresh pine filled the air along with the loamy scent of the earth that moved under my feet every time I swung the axe. As I tossed the fresh firewood on the pile, the sound of a car approaching made my ears perk up like I was a damn wolf or something. Bears didn't make cute little faces when they were listening or confused by something. There was no head tilting or wagging tails, and yes, I'd seen full-grown male shifters wagging their tails before when they wanted to get their point across. Bears were... grumpier. More solitary. More self-reliant and reserved. More *everything* really.

But I was a little biased.

Every shifter, even out of their fur, had better hearing than any human and was naturally stronger. It was part of what helped us stay hidden from prying eyes. So, when I was splitting wood for the fire, for example, I was able to do so at my own pace when I was alone but the moment, I sensed someone nearby I would drop the intensity with which I swung the ax to make it more believable that I was just a regular human. If I was feeling particularly indulgent, I may even swing so lightly that it took a couple of tries to break the wood apart, but that was only when I was pandering to someone.

A few minutes later, the sheriff's car pulled through the trees and parked in front of my place. "Howdy," I said as Sheriff Danvers got out of his cruiser. "What brings you this way?"

"Thought I'd stop in and say hello," Samuel said. He took his hat off and tossed it onto the passenger seat. I always hated that hat and having to wear it to be in proper uniform. The strange divots on the dome, the scratchy beige fabric, I hated all of it, but then I wasn't a huge fan of clothes in general, something I didn't have to worry about while in my bear skin.

When he looked back up at me, he put his thumbs around his belt and rested his hands there in a way that I'd only ever seen cops do. I knew part of it was ease of access to things they may need, but I couldn't help thinking part of it was because we all wanted to be the sheriff growing up, and probably watched more than one old spaghetti western. After an awkward pause, Samuel added, "I was in the area."

Sure. The area of my cabin that was out in the middle of the woods. He was in that area? Right.

I wouldn't push it though. Samuel clearly had something to talk to me about and he'd get to it in his own time. One thing I'd learned over the years was not to push. Sometimes the more you pushed the more people clammed up. Let them talk at their own pace and they might just spill their guts to you.

"Well come in, have some coffee." I stomped up the porch, knocking the mud and wood chips from my boots as I went, and held open the front door. I had a lady come in and clean often enough that it didn't bother me to have someone drop in. I wasn't otherwise much of a housekeeper on my own. I'd rather be out in the woods. Bear or human, I didn't mind, I just liked being in nature.

Part of the reason I lived all the way out here.

"Sit, sit." I motioned to the kitchen table while I grabbed a couple of mugs and poured out the coffee I always kept at the ready. "Black?"

"Of course," Samuel said, completely deadpan. "Milk is for sissies."

We shared a laugh as I sat across from him and sipped my coffee. Good thing I liked it black, too, or I might've been offended. Though we had both been on the force at the same time, we'd never really worked together outside of me being his boss while I was sheriff. It wasn't like he was a good friend stopping by to check on me.

"Been a rough week," Samuel said, running his hand over his thinning brown hair. "Real shame about Roger."

I nodded and grunted. "Very true. Ruled natural causes though, right?"

Samuel met my gaze, his dark eyes hard to read. "Well, as to that..."

"What?" I set my mug down and leaned forward. "Spit it out. You look like the cat that ate the canary."

Samuel sighed and set his mug down, too. "The thing is, Daniel, while Emma isn't a suspect anymore, I did have to do some digging on her while she was. I called around, spoke to the county PD back in Springfield where she was living, or is, since she hasn't technically moved to yet. Her ex-husband is missing as well. And so is the guy's new girlfriend."

I sat back in my seat and regarded the sheriff. He obviously thought Emma was up to some bad stuff. And in his shoes, I probably would have as well, only I knew Emma, and I knew there was no chance she'd do something like that.

"I'm just saying, Daniel, don't get distracted by a pretty face. I suspect this is all supernatural, and something you should handle, especially if Emma is an innocent party in it. I know you'll want to keep her safe. She doesn't seem like the type, but I can't deny that there's been some stranger than normal stuff happening since she turned up."

I wasn't sure how much he believed his own words that she could be innocent, but overall, he was right. Things had been a little extra odd since Emma came home, but I knew it wasn't her fault, the same way I knew I had to keep her safe.

My bear had begun pacing inside me, and I knew I'd have to check in on Emma sooner rather than later, just to make sure she was okay...if I wanted to get any sleep ever again. The idea of her being in danger just made everything I was already feeling more intense. But at the same time, I couldn't help but think about our last time together. In an ideal world, I'd avoid her until I felt less like a dumbass. But this wasn't an ideal world.

The sheriff tipped the plain white mug of coffee I'd given him up and drained it in two gulps, letting me know that he had done what he set out to do. With his obligations over with, I knew he wouldn't be hanging around to chat and catch up. That wasn't the kind of men we were. "Well, thanks for the coffee," Samuel said. "I didn't mean to barge in on you. I just didn't know how to get the bad news out."

We both stood and he pulled his belt and pants back up to where he thought they should be, as I said, "It's all right." I clapped him on the back and sighed, troubled about the news. "I'm glad you told me."

The two of us walked out and I went back to my wood-pile as though I was going to carry on with what I was doing now that he was leaving. I wasn't sure I could though. I watched him pull down my driveway as I thought about what I should do next. I wanted to call her local PD and find out what I could about her ex myself. She'd mentioned him, said their relationship had been rough at best. It seemed like an invasion of privacy though so I wasn't sure that would be the best step forward, not if I wanted to date her, which I did. I had no idea whether things between the two of us could work, but I knew if I didn't ask, if I didn't at least try, then I'd regret it.

I couldn't imagine her doing anything to hurt the man she'd clearly loved at one point in time, and especially not the new girlfriend. Emma might be angry and maybe even bitter, I wasn't sure, but I didn't think she'd hurt someone like that no matter how angry or hurt she was. Crimes of passion were... well, anyone could commit one, but still. Emma didn't seem the type to snap. If she was, then she would have snapped when she found out about the super-natural, right?

I couldn't pinpoint how I felt but confusion summed it up. I'd have to put in more thought about how to proceed.

Carefully, that was for sure. I didn't want Emma or myself to be set up for failure if we decided to try to do this. That meant figuring out what was going on without rocking the boat too much or making Emma doubt my intentions. It might be a bit like walking a tightrope, but it was a line that I'd gladly walk for her.

## 13

**Emma**

I'D NEVER BEEN AROUND WITCHES OTHER THAN MY FRIENDS, and even then, I hadn't been around all that much. Not recently, anyway, not since I knew they were witches, and not when they were being all magical. I'd never seen Deva make her food, only experienced it, and Beth's talking animals weren't a spell she had to cast or whatever, it was more like a forcefield around her, though I supposed she had got us into that nightclub when I was looking for Henry. I still wasn't clear on what she did there though. Carol was the only one I'd seen actively using magic when she was knitting, and she was the one who picked me up first thing the next morning. I hopped in the back seat as Deva, Carol, and Beth smiled and said their good mornings as I settled in next to Beth.

"Are you guys really okay with going?" I asked. They hadn't exactly seemed pleased when we realized that a witch might be behind this whole thing with Beth's ex and his business partner.

"Of course. Visiting the local coven is always fun." Carol backed out of my driveway and headed down the road.

"But you guys aren't in the coven, are you?" I asked.

They shook their heads almost in unison.

"Why aren't you, if you don't mind me asking?" I wasn't sure how they'd respond to the question. It's not like I expected my friends to be keeping secrets from me anymore, but they had kept the entire supernatural world a secret from me for years, so you know, it's not like there wasn't a precedence.

The car filled with an awkward silence. Finally, it was Beth next to me who huffed and said, "The coven is demanding. They require a lot of time and energy, which isn't something I could provide with raising Tiffany. Since I wasn't about to give up on raising her, I fell out of favor with the coven, and they never let me join as an adult." Guilt and frustration suffused her voice, and I couldn't help but reach out and take her hand in my own, squeezing it in support.

"I wouldn't have been able to give up on raising Henry if I was in the same situation."

"We didn't like how they treated Beth, so we chose to stick with our best friend and not a bunch of women we barely knew," Deva said, turning to grin at me from the front passenger seat.

"All for one and all that jazz," Carol said with a wink at me in the rearview mirror.

We pulled up at a stoplight, and I glanced over at one of the few restaurants with a drive-through. Some teen boys had just ordered, and they were all smirking, windows down, while one of them readied his phone, holding it out like a camera. My karma sense started to tingle, and my eyes narrowed. When they drove around to the window, the first guy was handed a giant shake. I pointed a finger at him as he opened the lid and threw it at the drive-through worker. Only, with karma doing its thing, the drink hit the side of the window and bounced back, soaking the whole inside of the car, and the jerks.

I could hear their howls of outrage. And the drive-through worker, a young girl, began to laugh hysterically, before slamming the window closed on them.

"Was that you?" Carol asked, and I could hear the amusement in her voice.

I shrugged. "They had it coming."

Everyone started laughing, and I felt glad that my powers could ease some of the tension we were all feeling. One day I'd have to ask them if life was this complicated before I came back into town, because if it was, their lives were pretty dang tough. And if it wasn't, I'd start to question if I'd brought more trouble into their lives than it was worth.

As the laughter died down, Carol started to talk, "I remember Bryan worked there in high school and he'd always tell me about--" she abruptly grew silent, and a pained look came over her face.

Beth and I exchange a look. We always suspected that the reason Carol had never gotten married, or even seemed to take an interest in dating, was because she'd never gotten over Bryan. Not that we blamed her. Out of all the kids in high school who dated people and seemed to think they'd always be together; Carol and Bryan were the only ones I thought were meant to be together.

But I'd heard, Bryan had simply left town one day with nothing more than a curt letter breaking up with her. He'd never explained why. And she'd been heartbroken.

"It's okay," Carol said, but her laugh lacked sincerity. "He was my high school boyfriend. I don't care about him anymore."

"It's alright if you still do," I said, gently.

"It'd be stupid to care about someone who couldn't so much as tell me goodbye in person." Her voice was firm, edged with anger.

"You're right," Deva forced out, a little too chipper. "Screw him!"

I frowned, an old memory surfacing. "Wasn't Bryan related to Cliff somehow?"

Darn it. I'd managed to make everyone uncomfortable again.

"Yeah," Carol said, softly. "He was."

She stopped talking. I looked at Beth, and she gently shook her head, so I knew it was time to shut up. I'd have to ask the others about the whole situation soon. But for now, we'd focus on figuring out which witch could possibly want revenge against Roger. And more about how witch magic could be used to kill someone.

A couple of minutes later, I knew we'd reached the right place. Surprisingly, the coven house was closer to mine than I expected, and yet, I wasn't sure I ever even knew there was a house over this way.

"I can't believe all this stuff went on right under my nose and I never even knew," I muttered as Carol turned up a long driveway. Halfway up it, a gate appeared from between two huge hedgerows ahead of us.

"To be fair, a lot of stuff is bespelled, so humans don't grow suspicious," Deva said with a shrug.

"Okay, that makes me feel *a little* less stupid," I muttered.

Carol smiled. "You were never stupid, Emma."

"You guys had to have been laughing at me at least a tiny bit in high school," I said.

"Never!" Deva exclaimed.

And, strangely, it made me feel a little better.

"If we could've told you, we would have," Carol reassured me.

"But now you're not getting rid of me," I said with a grin.

"Never!" They all said at the same time.

We kept going slowly toward the gate, but we didn't have to even roll down the window before the gate opened and Carol drove on through. I realized as we entered that the hedge wasn't just around the gate but around the entire property. It ran into the woods, or maybe around the woods as far as I could see on either side of the car. It explained why I'd never seen the house before. The thing was in no way, shape, or form visible from the road.

Around a couple more bends, the view opened with the ocean stretching on forever in the distance. The gigantic house was framed by trees and the insane view. In front of the house, a woman sat on a gold blanket reading. She looked like she'd come from a bygone age in a long white dress that had a high collar and sleeves that went down to her elbow, but even though it was conservative in most aspects it was nipped in at the waist, highlighting how tiny it was, and how curvaceous she was. The kicker was the way the skirt, which had a load of embroidery detail on it, was fanned out over the grass. All of that, combined with the way her hair was curled and pinned up, a few stray pieces waving in the breeze, made her breathtaking. She almost looked Edwardian with the dress and the way her hair was styled. I felt like someone should be painting her, she looked so picturesque.

We pulled onto a graveled area and parked. I felt insanely underdressed if this was how they rolled in the coven. She looked up as we walked past, but I was the only one who turned and waved at the beautiful woman. She winked at me, but didn't wave back, so at least she wasn't rude. I tugged on my flowy Rolling Stones t-shirt and pulled it down, so it covered more of my waist, not that it was a crop top or anything, but it only just met the waistband of my jeans, which now seemed like such a bad choice. I should have gone with a dress or something. I mean witches were always usually depicted that way, right? Although none of the witches I knew dressed like that, even now. Deva was in pants and a shirt, while Beth was in jeans and a t-shirt like me, though they looked nicer quality than mine. Carol was the only one in a skirt, but I knew that was just because she liked skirts, I mean, she wore mostly skirts and dresses so it would have been weird for her to show up in pants.

Deva knocked on the front door using the gigantic knocker and just like the gate, the door opened. A woman was heading toward the door as we walked into the big, cheery entryway. She was as opposite from the lady on the front lawn as she could've been. She wore a long, breezy, slightly wrinkled, tie-dyed dress with flowers woven into her hair and seemed to float, or glide, more than walk. Well, at least I didn't feel quite as underdressed anymore.

"Come in, please," the woman said. "I'm Hildy, and I'm a crystal witch, unusual I know but we're really just a subset of earth witches." She tossed her hair over her shoulder as though she'd just told us she was a unicorn, but since I had no idea what she was going on about, she just looked like any old horse to me. That was a little unfair, she didn't look like a horse, she was beautiful, just like the woman on the front lawn, but something about her personality made me feel a little sour toward her. She cleared her throat after clearly not getting the reaction she wanted and said, "Now, the gate wouldn't have opened if you all weren't some sort of witch." She looked at us with eyes sharper than her boho-hippy dress would've made her out to be. "I know you ladies." Hildy turned toward me, pinning me with her gaze as she seemed to assess me. "But you're new."

I nodded. "Yes, ma'am, I've only recently come into my, uh, powers."

She hummed and turned toward a big set of double doors that stood open. On the other side, two younger-looking witches wearing jeans and tees pointed their fingers at ping pong balls, which bounced into little plastic red cups. "Are they playing beer pong?" I asked with a laugh.

Hildy turned and smiled indulgently. "It helps our younger members practice their precision magic while still having fun. Follow me, please."

We walked through another room and a woman stood from a plush chair beside a mirror where another young witch studied herself. She snapped her fingers, and her outfit went from a casual cotton dress to a long, formal ball gown.

Hildy held out her hand and waved at the woman who had been observing the clothes changing. "Khat, would you care to join us?"

The older woman nodded as she looked our group over. "Of course. Deva, Carol, Beth, lovely to see you again." She walked toward us, but again it was more like she glided toward us, just like Hildy had.

"Tea, ladies?" Hildy asked.

No joke, a teapot, cups, saucers, a sugar bowl, and a little jug filled with milk came trotting out of a cabinet and over to the table where they floated up onto the wood surface before settling down like a cat in a sunbeam. If I didn't know better, I would think I was in a fairy tale or an enchanted castle.

"That would be lovely, thank you," Carol said as she sat on one of the wingback chairs that surrounded the coffee table.

The teapot poured itself into a cup and saucer that had set themselves up together and the sugar bowl and milk jug went waddling over to the cup. Carol picked up two sugar cubes and dropped them into the steaming liquid before adding a splash of milk. The steam that rose after that formed a heart shape and she smiled down at it before looking back up at us.

I was pretty sure my jaw was hanging open.

Birds chirping drew my attention away from my friend for a moment and though I saw them, they weren't what I expected. All kinds of finches, sparrows, and bluebirds hopped around, but they were inside the wallpaper. The trees were obviously painted or illustrated somehow but the birds looked completely lifelike. It made me rethink that short story about yellow wallpaper I'd read in my English Lit class.

Khat opened a door to a sitting room and the coffee table and wingback chair holding Carol began to shuffle into the room both with a surprisingly graceful gate that didn't spill a drop of tea from the pot or Carol's cup. I wanted to ask if I'd accidentally taken drugs before we came over, that was how bizarre it all was, but when Carol grinned knowingly at me, seeming perfectly at ease being carried by her chair as she went by sipping on her tea, I knew I was stone-cold sober.

Once we had followed Carol and Khat in, I could see that the sitting room had no birds in the wallpaper and no tiny doorways for anything to come in or go out. In fact, the only way into and out of the room was the door we'd all just filed through, which, for some reason, made me uneasy. "Now," Khat said. "What can we do for you?"

"We need some help, if possible," Carol said. I'd noticed that she sort of took the lead with the witches, whereas Deva was quiet, and Beth was practically nonexistent at my side, which was unusual for her. I reached out and clasped her hand in my own, giving it a squeeze of support and encouragement as Carol said, "We need to find out if there was any major magic done on a specific night."

Khat flicked her finger and the teapot poured tea for the rest of us as we all sat down in the chairs that were already in the room. I'm not going to lie though, the idea that the chair under me could come to life had me perching on the very edge, ready to jump up at any second.

Hildy pushed her curly hair out of her eyes. "Well, it's doable." She and Khat exchanged a look, but I had no idea what it meant.

Khat arched an eyebrow at us and said, "But you'd better be prepared for whatever we find." I knew that they meant to be kind with their warning, but we weren't exactly in a place where we could rethink things. We needed answers, and if they had a way of providing them then I'd take whatever the consequences were.

Apparently, we all felt the same because we all nodded in unison. "We just need to get to the bottom of all this," Deva said, glancing worriedly at Beth who was barely even looking up from her cup of tea. There had been no steam heart for her, or me for that matter. I wondered what it meant, probably nothing, just the teapot being weird, I mean the thing could walk and act on its own so who knew what the steam might do.

"Finish your tea," Khat said, her eyes gentle, but her mouth drawn into a thin line. "And then, we begin."

Begin? How exactly would we find the answers we sought?

I had a feeling things were about to get even weirder.

## 14

**Emma**

"Come on," Carol said, smiling at me. "I think you're in for a treat."

We all stood and walked away from the tea, which had been delicious, with my curiosity piqued. "What kind of treat?" Part of me hoped it was food. All the intensity I'd been feeling when it came to visiting the witches and being by Beth's side and protecting her was giving me a serious case of stress snacking. The problem was I had nothing to snack on. At this point I'd even take those crackers that my mom used to give me when I was sick that were basically cardboard with some salt on them.

Deva turned and grinned at me, her eyes twinkling. "I know for a fact there's no way you've ever done this before."

"What?" For some reason, they all seem a little too pleased with themselves for my liking.

"Fly," she said, softly. If someone had hit me with a feather at that moment, they probably could have knocked me over.

Fly? As in they plan to make us all sprout wings? Or were we being turned into birds? I swear I read a book once where they were turned into birds and flew to the south pole. I really didn't want to have to fly all the way to the south pole, or the north pole. No matter where we were going, I was pretty sure I'd prefer to take a car. Not that I would say that in front of the strange witches. Who knew what could piss them off?

I realized that they were all leaving without me, while I stood in stunned silence, and hurried to catch up to the group as they walked through the foyer again and across the house. I managed to catch up to them in the kitchen. "Um, flying?" I finally managed weakly.

Beth laughed and grabbed my hand. "Come on!" It was the first time I'd really seen her look happy in the last twenty-four hours, especially since we'd come to see the witches. She'd been so much more withdrawn than normal. It was like she took the fact that they didn't let her join as a judgement on her as a person, which I didn't think was fair. If anything, it made them look unreasonable and a little snobby. Not that I would ever say that out loud.

Once we walked out the back door, I quickly realized what they had in mind. A row of brooms leaned up against the back of the house. All sorts of brooms. Tall ones with long, feathery brushes and shorter ones with flat bottomed brushes, ones made of every kind of wood, and even some painted elaborate colors. It looked like I'd stepped into some kind of strange art gallery, every exhibit featuring different types of brooms. It was odd. But apparently, everything was a little odd about the supernatural world.

Including me.

"Your broom will determine what sort of ride you have,"

Beth explained. "A soft broom gives a cushier ride. A more industrial type of broom will be fast and efficient."

"So, I'm looking for a soft broom," I said.

My friends were all grinning.

Carol pointed to a sleek one. "You sure you aren't looking for a smooth ride that will get you to where you want to go *fast*."

I looked at her and my jaw dropped open. "Are you making a sexual joke?"

She pointed to one that's bumpy, crooked, and looked like it was made of splinters. "I would stay away from that one. You've already had your share of terrible rides."

I couldn't help it, I burst out laughing.

Deva leaned in. "She making sex jokes about brooms again?"

I nodded, feeling stupid.

Deva shook her head, but she was smiling. "Good old Carol, still the same as when we were teens."

"Who are you calling *old*," she said, heading for the brooms.

With a chuckle, I grabbed a broom that reminded me of what my grandmother had used, with long straw pieces on the end. If I was looking for something that would be slow and steady, I had a feeling this would be the perfect match. "How about this?"

"A good choice," Deva said. "That broom should definitely be a good ride for a beginner. You ready to try this?"

My nerves jangled, but I nodded. "I am."

Why not? I trusted my friends not to get me hurt. I wasn't at all sure why we needed to fly or where to, but who was I to turn down an adventure like this?

A tiny thought strays to my perfectly dependable car. It wasn't fancy and new like Rick's and it wasn't brightly colored either, but it was stalwart. I knew I had a few more years before things really started to go wrong with it, much like myself. I was creaking here and there, but if I treated myself right then I would have some time before I started feeling like I was completely falling apart, or at least that was my hope.

The old Emma would've never done this. But the old Emma was trapped in a miserable marriage, feeling alone in a quiet house, with the weight of the world on her shoulders. The old Emma felt like she was in a slow marathon that only ended with death.

I definitely preferred the side of me that had real friends and a real life. The side of me that tried to be brave and took on the world, rather than hiding from it. So, if riding a broom was my next challenge, I'd try to face it with the same kind of grace as the group of friends I admired so much.

"We prefer traveling this way," Khat said, as if she knew the questions that had been running through my mind. "We do it whenever we can. And it's so much faster than walking to the woods where we need to go to do this spell."

"Is there any trick to it?" I asked, imagining myself flying straight into the sun, or turning into one of those Halloween decorations where the witch and her broom are wrapped around a tree, like they hit it.

Beth giggled. "Nope. Just hop on and push off. The brooms are spelled. You can't fall off unless someone curses you off."

Each of us chose a different kind of broom. Carol, to my surprise, chose the super sleek one that almost looked like it was made from a dark brown metal. Deva chose one that was... pretty. It had been painted a sky blue and had feathers instead of straw at the bottom of it. The emerald, gold, and sapphires made them look like peacock feathers, which somehow suited Deva. But Beth, she seemed to choose the one closest to her with little thought. It was plain-looking, but with little carvings in the handle, and seemed sturdy enough.

Each of the ladies climbed onto their brooms, and then Khat and Hildy both chose ones nearly as sleek as the one Carol had chosen. They seemed comfortable with their brooms, so I suspected they were brooms they often rode. It made me feel a little like I'd joined a class for horseback riding, only to discover I was the only newcomer. But they said I couldn't fall off unless cursed, so I hoped I'd be okay.

With my stomach jumping, I swung my foot over the handle of my broom and looked at my friends, feeling uncertain. "Um..."

"Jump!" Deva yelled as she did exactly as she said. As she rose into the air, Carol followed quickly behind as our hosts hovered near the ground. Hildy was riding in a way that was essentially sidesaddle, so the broom didn't push up her skirt. For some reason I hadn't expected her to care.

I stood for a long minute studying them hovering in the air. None of them looked the least bit scared. In fact, they looked excited. And that alone was enough to ease a bit of my anxiety. Surely if this was terrifying, they wouldn't be so quick to do it again, right?

"You ready?" Beth asked.

Psyching myself up, I did a countdown in my head, squealed as I squatted down, and then jumped into the air. The hard, wooden handle took my weight right between my legs. It didn't hurt, but it wasn't exactly pleasant either. I had a moment of wondering if riding sidesaddle was more comfortable. I was far too nervous about rapidly rising into the air to fully notice if straddling a broom was going to end up painful after a few minutes, but I guess I'd jump that hurdle when I came to it. I felt more like I was holding my breath, trying to decide at which height I should start freaking the heck out.

I followed my friends and the two witch hosts over an expanse of trees. None of us were going too high, just above the trees, and... it felt amazing. The wind was whipping all around me, like when I would unroll all my car windows and drive down a slowly winding road. Only, this was even better. Part of me wanted to stick and arm out and roll one of my hands through the air, like I did with the car window. It was like I could taste the cleanest air imaginable, like I was actually some kind of fantastical creature that had grown wings and taken off into the sky.

It was truly incredible, so when I pointed the tip of the broom down and I started to slide, I didn't expect it. Screaming out, I gripped the broom as hard as I could and squawked for my friends. "Beth!"

She pulled up on her broom handle and chuckled. "You won't fall off!"

I wasn't so sure about that, but I was not pointing my broom down for a while. And the pleasant experience I was having just a minute ago? The feeling had all but disappeared. Now, I was just tightly gripping the broom and hoping like mad we reached wherever we were going as soon as possible.

After a few minutes, Hildy waved toward the ground, and all the women pointed their brooms down and started to descend. For a minute, I didn't do anything. I just stared down at the trees and remembered that feeling, like I was falling.

"You can't stay up here forever," Carol said, with a laugh.

Deva looked back at me and gave a reassuring smile. "You'll be okay. I promise."

I took a deep breath and just slightly tilted the handle down. This time, the descent didn't feel quite as much like I was going to fly off and fall to my death. So, with my sweaty hands tightly gripping the wooden handle, I gritted my teeth and focused on the little clearing, which seemed to be our goal. The wind plucked at me a bit, making my descent not nearly as smooth as my flight, but I just kept focusing. Hoping and praying jumping on a broom and flying wouldn't be the last adventure I ever had.

After what felt like forever, I landed beside Deva with my hair no doubt frazzled and flying everywhere. I dropped the broom on the ground and stepped back from it like it was a snake, before wiping my sweaty palms on my pants and trying to fix my crazy hair.

"Don't worry, you look... nice," Deva said, noticing my struggles.

I glared at her and her short, perfect hair. "Next time, I'm cutting my hair first."

"Oh, I know the perfect person to do your hair!" she said, far too excited.

I lifted a brow. "Uh, do you not like my hair?"

She shrugs. "I like it. But you've been wearing it that way since we were kids. Maybe it's time for a change."

She had a point there. Breathing deeply, more like I'd run to the woods instead of flying, I realized that the other ladies had all gone to sit in the grass in a circle. So, I hurried forward to sit beside Khat and Hildy. After all, we weren't here to learn about witches and brooms, we were here to protect Beth. I couldn't forget that.

"What do I do?" I whispered as Beth completed the circle.

"Nothing," Hildy said. "Just join hands. I will complete the spell and draw power from you if I need it."

"Draw power from me? Will that hurt?"

She lifted a brow, and her eyes seemed to twinkle. "No. It never hurts. But for someone as powerful as you? It shouldn't even make you tired."

"How do you know I'm powerful?"

"I know a lot of things," she said mysteriously, then stretched out one of her hands toward me and the other to Khat who sat on Hildy's other side.

Okay. So, this wasn't going to hurt, and I just had to hold her hand? I could do that. I flew on a damn broom, challenged sirens, and raised a son. Holding hands with a weird witch? Easy enough. Could've been a lot worse.

Hildy sucked in a deep breath and she looked like she was completely in her element. Her flowing skirt was spreading out around her, and her blonde hair fell wildly around her shoulders, but in a way that was pretty, versus my hair, which probably looked like it was attacked by a weed whacker. What's more, she just seemed... peaceful. I imagined that she never felt more like herself than when she was with nature. Kind of how I felt when I was in my parent's house.

"Great Mother Earth," she began. "We call upon you in an hour of need, to reveal the secrets of our world. Secrets that could be dangerous. We call upon you to help channel our powers and show us what we need to know."

I looked at Beth, about to mutter something about this whole thing being weird, but her gaze was locked on Hildy, so I shut up and looked back at the witch. For a long time, nothing happened, we just sat in silence, and then I felt something, like a tingle, moving through my hand where I was connected to Hildy. At first, I wasn't sure if it was connected to all of this, but then the tingly feeling increased until it was almost uncomfortable.

A strange sense, that we were all connected, rushed over me. I swore I could hear all their heartbeats beating in tune with mine, and our breaths were all measured and controlled together. It wasn't like I was sliding into their bodies, but more so that we were connected in a way I could never imagine. And then, that feeling grew, and suddenly I was overwhelmed by the scents of the forest. Pine filled my nostrils, and the wind seemed to wrap around my skin. I could feel each tree gently moving with the breeze, and all the plants bending under its force. It even felt like I was aware of every single animal in the woods around us.

And then, for one terrible moment, it was like I was that in tune with the whole world. With every living person. With every plant and creature. I was lost for a minute, no longer a person, but a vessel.

I almost said it was too much, that I couldn't handle anymore, when it abruptly ended.

This time... I felt alone. So alone that tears filled my eyes, and my chest felt heavy with a need to sob and sob into the sky, to reach out for all the living things that I was briefly connected to.

But Hildy fell over, drawing me back to reality in an instant. Her friend, Khat, lurched forward and tried to help, but Hildy's eyes rolled up in her head and she twitched. It was as if whatever spell she'd created was too much for her body, and it scared me. Was this supposed to happen? Or had something gone wrong?

I looked at the others. They all seemed worried, which told me that this wasn't normal. And that deep sense of worry grew deeper inside of me. This seemed like the best choice to discover who was after Beth, but what if we'd hurt someone for the information? I wasn't sure I could forgive myself.

"What's wrong with her?" I gasped.

Deva yanked something out of her pocket. "Here." She handed Khat a little piece of candy. "That will give her strength."

Khat stuffed the candy in Hildy's mouth and looked back at Deva with uncertainty, but Deva nodded her on as she said, "Massage her throat."

A few seconds later, Hildy calmed down and blinked at us as she struggled to sit up. "Oh, my," she whispered. "That was intense."

Intense? Okay, so none of this was normal, but she seemed okay now. So, what did she mean by intense?

She breathed deep and took another piece of candy from Deva, who apparently had a whole stash in her pocket. "Thank you, dear. Your candy really helped me break away."

"Away from what?" I squeaked.

Hildy looked at Beth with grave eyes. "The force that held me... it must be destroyed, or I fear it will destroy you."

*Uh oh.*

Beth's cheeks paled as she absorbed Hildy's words.

"Can we find the source?" Deva asked, and even though she was hard to rattle, she seemed shaken, almost scared.

Actually, the whole group seemed upset. So, what did all this mean?

Khat held Hildy's hands as the witch nodded. "I believe we can find the source and save Beth, but the cost may be great."

# 15

## Emma

THE NIGHT AIR WAS COLD, AND THE WIND CARRIED WITH IT the scents of the forest, of green life and nature, but there was also another scent, one that felt like magic. Or, maybe, I was only imagining the sweet and spicy something that whispered that it was supernatural. Yet, every time I took a deep breath, I couldn't shake the sense that this night held the possibility of incredible things.

In front of me, a bonfire blazed. The dancing flames illuminated the trees in a way that was some mix of frightening and liberating. Kind of like how every day had been since becoming Karma. With each leap of the flames, the shadows danced around us, and it made it feel like the man who attacked us could be feet from us, and we'd never even know. Sometimes I even imagined eyes watching me from the dark, but I tried to push away the silly fear. Instead, I focused on the fire, but I couldn't shake free of what I was about to do. In a lot of ways, it was the most terrifying thing I've done since coming back to Mystic Hollow.

Which was silly. I'd been through so much craziness. And yet, it didn't change the way I felt.

Gulping, I did everything I could to calm my heart rate. Breathing evenly, I wiggled my toes in the grass, enjoying the feel of the dampness of the soil. I was safe. I had no reason to be so terrified. And I was a logical person. Wasn't I?

A hand on my back gently pushed me forward. As I stepped lightly over the grass, I looked back at Beth's smiling face. She winked at me from under her hooded robe. I wore one just like it, as did Deva and Carol, and a whole bunch of nameless witches from the coven. To them, all of this was normal. But to me, it was like standing up in front of a crowd and singing, with my awful singing voice. Or, maybe, diving off the edge of a cliff and just hoping I don't come down on a rock... or two inches of water.

What was coming made my stomach churn. But I simply had to do it. I had to help Beth figure out what was going on before she was hurt by all this insanity. And they had all assured me this was the only way. So, this would just be the next thing that the "new" me would do. I just hoped no one else could tell just how nervous I was.

Without warning, someone pulled on my robe, yanking it off my back.

A small squeak left my lips, and my hands flew to cover my most important parts. I spun back to see Carol behind me, looking pleased with herself.

Then, all my friends dropped their robes too, along with the other witches. And, yeah, we were all standing around naked. This wasn't even like when I had to get naked in the locker room in high school. As embarrassed as I had been then, my boobs weren't pancakes back then, my butt round and low, and my belly covered in stretch marks. Now, I had something to be self-conscious about.

"There ya' go," Carol finally said with laughter in her voice. "The first time is the hardest."

Someone began singing, an old song, acapella, as the women from the coven began to dance. And it was strange. Suddenly, I realized that no one was staring at me. No one was whispering behind their hands about old pancake boobs. They were just... dancing. Dancing as if no one was watching. Dancing, their arms waving above their bodies, and their hips swinging like there wasn't a thing in the world wrong about dancing naked in the woods.

I had the strangest moment when all of this felt normal.

It was official. I'm losing my mind.

"Come on," Deva whispered as she took my hand. "Just focus on the magic and the stars. You'll forget you're naked soon."

I tried to do as she said and to my utter shock, she was right. As easy as it had been to see the other women looking so free, it quickly became easy for me too. Soon I was humming along, the tune quickly becoming a part of me, pounding through my blood and heart as my magic pulsed out of me and joined the collective magic of the group.

Because that was exactly what was happening now. Our magic was dancing together. Each of us radiated a different color, a light that was more subtle than the light from the flames, but the colors lifted above our heads, moving above us like smoke with a mind of its own. The colors began to swirl together, joining, and the cloud group bigger. My own color, to my surprise, was a lovely purple, like lavender. And as I stared at it, spinning around, my heart swelled. Lavender. It was a good color. A color I was proud of.

Carol's magic seemed to be a subtle mix of colors, unlike

most of the other women. Her colors reminded me of her knitting projects. Even the thought made me smile. Beth's was a bright pink, no surprise there. It reminded me of her personality. She'd always had the best smile. The biggest personality. She was bright pink, inside, and out. Deva's, on the other hand, was a soft blue. No less beautiful than the pink, but it captured her in a way that made tears gather in my eyes.

There were so many colors. So much magic gathered together. It made me feel this deep sense that every person in the world had a color, like their aura, or their soul, and that every color was beautiful in its own way.

My gaze met with Beth's, and there were tears in her eyes. I wondered, since she wasn't allowed to join the coven, if she was just overwhelmed by emotions too. Or if it was because she was afraid of what she might learn tonight.

Unable to help myself, I went and snagged her hands. We spun together like children, and she smiled, even as her tears finally escaped and rolled down her cheeks. I felt myself crying too, but it was like my soul was just that happy.

The clearing began to feel heavy. Like a roof filling with steam. I glanced up at the cloud above us, and it almost blocked out the sky. Only the moon still peeked through the rainbow of dancing colors. I held my breath, feeling like we were on the edge of something powerful.

Suddenly, a harsh voice filled the clearing. We stopped dancing and whirled around to find Hildy standing with her arms spread in the air.

My heart raced. A coldness I didn't understand rolled down my spine, and I felt the mood of the women around me change. The colors above us exploded out, and cold wind rushed toward us, nearly putting out the bonfire. A few tiny flames and embers remained, but otherwise, we were swallowed in darkness.

Everyone seemed to be holding their breaths.

Hildy walked over the hot coals and came to stand in the middle of them, not even wincing. Her gaze was focused above her, at the moon, and her arms remained spread wide. Her body jerked a couple of times, and then she crumbled to her knees, and the remaining flames were quenched, as embers rose up around the witch. "The missing man has returned," Hildy said, her voice guttural and hard to understand. "He's no longer human."

Beth gasped, and my chest felt tight. I stepped back and put my arm around her shoulders, not even caring that we were both naked. The missing man wasn't human? That couldn't be good.

Hildy continued as all the embers fell and disappeared, "The only way to stop him is to find the person who did the first spell. He or she must undo it, or Beth will never be free."

"Who did the spell?" Deva called, sounding upset.

With her eyes closed, Hildy looked at Deva. Creepy. "They are not of our coven. They are rogue."

A rogue witch? Was that common? Was that something my friends would know how to handle?

Hildy fell on her side, and a couple witches rushed forward and drew her from the ash. They wrapped her in a robe, and then everyone began to dress. A somberness had fallen over us all. Apparently, as amazing as it was to connect my magic with other women, the truth has a way of destroying that feeling of happiness inside of me.

My friends and I grabbed our robes and covered up. I could barely see them in the darkness, but I could sense their grim moods. Smoke hung in the air, hung over us all, blocking out the scents of nature and of fresh air. It was as if a switch had been flipped and everything was different.

Clearly, the night was done. The magic had disbursed, and now we knew. The danger for Beth had become a concrete thing. A concrete person we had to find, in order to keep her safe. And whatever we had to do, we had to do it soon.

Or we could lose Beth. And I wouldn't lose her, no matter what it cost me.

## 16

**Daniel**

THE RINGING PHONE CUT THROUGH THE HARSH SILENCE OF THE cabin. I hadn't been home long. I hadn't even turned on the TV, which I tended to keep on for a bit of noise in the background. I didn't mind being alone, I was used to it, but sometimes the silence was too much, at least inside the cabin. Outside it wasn't so bad, the birds were singing, critters were foraging, and all that. Inside was just too still and quiet for my liking, hence the TV.

I pressed the speaker button as I passed by my phone on the coffee table, tossing a couple of logs into the wood burning stove that sat in the corner. I didn't use it as a stove anymore, but it kept the place nice and toasty. "Yeah?" I swung the cast iron door shut and locked it, opening the vent at the top a little more, so the heat got out, but the smoke went up the chimney.

"Daniel?"

"Hey, Samuel, how's it going?" I grabbed my phone and carried it across the small area of the cabin. The area between the kitchen and the living space was where I had my dining table, which was generally where guests like Samuel sat when they dropped by for coffee. Not many people liked to sit in front of the TV, I wasn't sure why, maybe they felt awkward seeing their reflection in the empty black screen, or maybe it was because there was only the two-seater and an armchair. I passed by the wood table and moved into the kitchen, setting the phone on the counter so I could keep chopping vegetables to make a stew. It wasn't fancy, but it was tasty and filling which were both important things. Plus, it was a good way to get my vegetables in and not just wind up being a meat and potatoes kind of guy.

"You're still hanging around with Emma Pierce, aren't you?" Samuel asked. His question was innocuous but there was something in his tone that suggested he thought that there was something more going on between us than there currently was.

I grabbed another carrot and nodded as I replied, the thought of Emma bringing a smile to my face. "Yes, why?" I topped and tailed it, giving it a quick scrub before I began chopping. My mom always told me that most of the nutrients were in the peel, that may have been an old wives' tale, or may have just been that she didn't want to waste time peeling vegetables, but I stuck to it, just in case.

"Detective Morris, from Springfield police department has been assigned the case involving the disappearance of Emma's ex-husband," he paused, and I could tell he was looking at his notes, even if I hadn't heard the rustle of the notepad pages turning. "Like we discussed before, it isn't that Ms. Pierce is a suspect, but the longer they're gone, the more suspicious it looks. Since you started spending time with her, has she discussed anything about her ex with you?

"She hasn't mentioned anything." Not that we'd really spent a lot of time discussing her ex-husband. "And I can't see her having anything to do with it."

"Okay, I guess that's good. The detective did say they're prone to up and take trips out of the blue, but it's been a while and his office is getting concerned, so they're looking into it." Samuel sighed and paused for a beat before he added, "I'm sure they'll turn up. These rich folks always forget that someone is relying on them for things. Apparently, they need him to sign some paperwork or something, and they're running out of time. I don't know, it's all paper pusher stuff that I try and avoid."

"I'm sure they'll turn up, as you said. Probably just gone off for a getaway or something."

Samuel made a noise that could have been agreement, could have been annoyance, could have been pretty much anything since it was just a grunt. He was the type of man that would lay it all out there if he had a question that needed answering though, not the type to beat around the bush.

"Some neighbors also mention that the divorce didn't seem to be amicable. That they heard some arguing and that the husband was not going to make it an easy process. There's also a strong suggestion that his current relationship had been started during the marriage..."

"Well, people talk," I told him, trying to choose my words carefully.

He sighed. "Okay, then, I guess if she mentions anything, give me a call. Even if it's just a place the two might have gone. I think the detective was a little annoyed having to waste his time on something like this, and we both know how those kinds of cases are."

"Yeah." I did. Most missing people were missing because

they didn't want to be found for a little while. Not all of them. But every cop preferred a case where a missing person was just inconsiderate, or too dumb, to make sure the people around them knew where they were, rather than something awful happening to a person.

"Well, goodbye, back to keep an eye on the streets."

I smiled. "Goodbye."

After we hung up and I was through making my stew, all I could think about was Emma. She was mercurial but in a good way. I never knew what to expect from her, and ever since she'd come back to town things had been interesting to say the least. When she'd made the water at the falls flow again, I thought I was going to faint, and the way she cared about Henry, she was clearly a dedicated woman. If Rick had done something to hurt her before they split, then I'd have a hard time not going after him myself. The fact that he'd let a woman like Emma slip through his fingers told me everything I needed to know about him. And the fact that he had a new girlfriend when I wasn't even sure the divorce was final?

I knew exactly what kind of man he was. Wasteful, power hungry, unscrupulous, with a cold heart. After all, Emma was the mother of his child, and from my understanding they only had the one.

Part of me couldn't help but wonder what Emma's kid was like, even though he wasn't really a kid anymore, since he had to be away at college at the least if Emma was here alone. Had she raised the boy more in her image or did he take after his dad. Did he call her? Did she miss him?

That last one was a dumb question, of course she missed her only child. Somehow, I don't think I would assume the same about her ex though. Letting your wife, who seemed to be amazing to me, go, no, not just letting her go, but walking away from her? It was the move of someone who didn't care about much of anything other than themselves.

Of course, there were instances where people fell out of love with one another, where divorce was what was best for both of them, but the way Emma talked about Rick? I didn't get the impression that she had fallen out of love with him, not until he'd yanked her heart from her chest and stomped on it.

Why did I want to be the one to repair it? My own heart was still damaged after everything that happened with Sarah. How could I repair something that was broken for someone else when I couldn't even fix it for myself?

Maybe we didn't need to be fixed though. Maybe we were fine as we were and our broken pieces could fit together, bring us closer. I pushed the thought away.

Sarah had been gone a long time and I had dated since, but there was something about Emma that was different. Something about her, and the way I felt about her, scared me when it came to taking the next step, and I wasn't a man that was easily scared.

After dinner, enough was enough. I wanted to call her; the goofy, silly woman who never failed to make me smile. God when she came running down the stairs with that underwear on her head the last time I was over, I thought I was going to lose it. She'd clearly fussed with her hair as well to get it to stand up like that. Her face when she saw me was a picture, and the blush that rose on her cheeks from being caught was more than a little enticing. There was no way she could've done something to hurt her ex. The woman I knew just wasn't capable of it.

As I considered calling to ask Emma out on a date, something made my sixth sense tingle. My bear senses were heightened and going off like crazy. Something was happening outside.

With a growl, I flung open my front door. I was one of the biggest, baddest shifters on the Eastern Seaboard. It wasn't likely to be something that could take me out. It was something that needed to learn some damn manners, and to stay off my property. A lesson it was going to learn very quickly if it wanted to stay alive.

As I stepped off my front porch, my instincts going wild, I had to prepare to shift. There was something out here that needed taking care of. I wasn't about to let anyone roam my land unchecked.

## 17

**Emma**

WHEN I GOT BACK FROM DANCING NAKED IN THE WOODS, I found a very exhausted-looking Henry and Alice. Henry was wearing his favorite pajamas, with video game characters on them. And Alice was wearing a zip-up onesie with anime characters smiling from the pink fabric. They were both taking their vitamins in the kitchen and seemed to be ready for bed.

Henry nodded at me when I came in. "Long night?"

I sighed. "Yeah. Kind of. What about you guys?"

"We finally managed to take the castle and win the Sword of Justice." He looked over at Alice with a smile. "I gave it to her, of course. It was her plan, after all, that allowed us to win over the reapers."

Alice's dark eyes gave Henry a gentle look, then she glanced at me, a slight frown pulling at the edges of her lips. "I don't think Emma's in the mood to talk about a video game right now. She's had a rough night. Her nerves are fried, and she's scared."

I stiffened, surprised. "How do you know that?"

Henry looked at Alice. "I told you, Emma is supernatural now. We can trust her if you want to. It's your choice."

Alice ran a hand through her auburn locks, avoiding my gaze and chewing her bottom lip. It was the first time I'd seen her hair out of the tight bun she liked to wear it in, and I was a little surprised by the fact that she looked a little older and strikingly beautiful. "I'm an empath," she finally managed.

"An empath?" I thought I'd heard something about that before.

She nodded. "I can sense what other people are feeling."

"Wow, that's an amazing gift," I said, without thinking.

Alice winced. "It can be, but it's mostly a curse. It gets exhausting to constantly feel what other people are feeling. I used to try to stay home and away from my parents as much as I could. But when I met Henry... everything changed. His emotions are so controlled. If he's upset, he doesn't brew and brew over it. He tells me, and then his emotions decrease and fade. Being around him is almost as good as being alone. Better, if you add how nice it is to be with him," she said with a smile.

Henry returned her smile. "And Alice never gets mad that I don't show my emotions more. She likes me exactly how I am."

I felt tears burn my eyes. "I'm so happy for both of you."

Alice reached out and gently squeezed my arm. "I heard that maybe something might be going on between Daniel and you. I think he would be a good choice for you. His emotions are well controlled, for a shifter. He's kind and understanding. I know most of the people in this town better than they know themselves, and Daniel is one of the good ones. He was broken for a long time after his wife died, but I think he's ready for love now."

I felt a blush warm my cheeks. Did *everyone* know about Daniel and me?

"It's time for bed," Henry said.

I wished them a good night, then went to take a shower, washing away the night the best way I could. When I was done, the water had long ago become cold. I dressed but still didn't feel tired. So, I quietly went to the kitchen, made myself some tea, and sat on the couch, playing a dumb game where I crush cookies or candies. Something like that. By the time I was out of lives, it was ridiculously late.

Tiptoeing through the house, I checked the locks on the doors. Henry was sound asleep, judging from the snores coming from his room. The guy was practically a cartoon when it came to the sounds he made while he was asleep. Deep snorts followed by high-pitched whines were the most common sounds. It half made me wonder if he should see a sleep specialist or something. And because I heard nothing from their room, I assumed Alice was asleep as well.

Good, they deserved to be able to relax and rest.

I moved away from Henry's room and went to check the sliding door at the back of the house. It was the one he usually forgot to lock. Walking around the house in the middle of the night after coming back from dancing naked in the woods felt odd. Part of me wanted to dance the night away, to watch the magic that was swirling out from the witches and myself for forever, but then I'd remember what Hildy had said about Beth never being free and my heart turned into a block of ice in my chest.

The lock on the sliding door was down and the length of wood that sat on the runner to prevent it from being opened if someone were able to pick the lock, or something, was there as well. A thought occurred to me that the house wasn't protected from any kind of magical attacks. There were magical attacks, right? I'd have to talk to the ladies about that. Surely there were protective charms or whatever that we could put on the house itself? Then I realized that I was thinking about someone attacking me and my brother, in our home, with magic. What was this crazy world I'd fallen into?

I mean, really. Who lived this way?

I had to admit it was freeing though, knowing what was out there and what I was and could do. It made me feel powerful. I did a little twirl just like I'd done when I'd been dancing under the moonlight a few hours ago and it was like my body remembered the magic. I was light and almost carefree, even after getting such grave news. I turned off the kitchen light and headed toward the stairs once more, my mind finally at ease now that I knew we were locked in and safe.

A knock on my door made my blood run cold. Who would be here this late?

Peering carefully out of the peephole, I sighed in relief when I caught Daniel's profile in the moonlight. But he held his arm funny. And definitely not funny as in haha. There was no Ministry of Strange Arm Holding as far as I knew, just Silly Walks. As fast as I could, I unlocked the door.

As soon as I had it open wide enough, I shot my hand out and grabbed the arm that he wasn't holding strangely and pulled him inside. "What's wrong?" I hissed, not wanting to wake Henry and Alice and deal with that conversation.

Daniel grunted as I touched him. "Careful."

"Come sit." I closed the door behind us and made sure it was locked and the chain was on. No one was getting in this house without us knowing about it. Using his good elbow to guide him I walked us over to the couch. Daniel wasn't moving as fast as usual, and I had to wonder if something was wrong with one of his legs as well as his arm. Finally, he kind of fell onto the couch instead of sitting down. I sat down next to him and started to look him over, trying to figure out what I'd need from the medicine cabinet.

"I'm okay," he said. "Don't fuss. I'll be healed in another hour, but I had to come make sure you were okay."

"Was this one of the wolves?" I asked, my anger rising. "Did they attack you?"

He shook his head and grimaced as I gently prodded his shoulder. "No, this thing wasn't any shifter I've ever seen. For one, it didn't attack the way a shifter would with claws and teeth. It was more of a blunt force. And it was dark and moved so fast, I couldn't really tell what the hell it was."

"Did you call the sheriff?" I asked. I wasn't sure what the sheriff could do, but it seemed like he should at least be aware that there was a vicious shifter roaming around, one that was willing to take on a guy as big as a full-grown male bear.

Daniel laid his head against the couch and sighed, his breathing slightly labored, which worried me. "Yeah. Listen, Emma, I don't want to scare you, and I can't fully explain how I know this, but I'm pretty sure it's not really a shifter, it's something similar but there's just something off about it."

"Like you sensed it?" I asked. "Some sort of preternatural thing?"

He shrugged and winced. "I don't know. But it, or he, or whatever, got away from me."

Daniel looked so sad I shifted closer to him on the couch, and he turned to look at me, suddenly bringing us closer than we'd ever been "Hey," I whispered. "It's okay. I'm just glad you're not hurt. And as you can see, I'm fine."

His sage green eyes softened as he leaned forward. I couldn't help but focus on his lips, my heart pounding with anticipation of how they'd feel pressed against mine. He had full lips. When we'd been in high school together, I'd had many, many dreams about them and what kissing him would be like. My breath hitched as he got closer, and my heart practically skipped in my chest. I wasn't sure whether it was from nervousness or excitement.

My breath caught in my throat as my phone squawked from my pocket, playing an obnoxious country song that Deva had set for her ringtone as a joke. Lurching out of my seat, I ignored Daniel's soft curse and yanked my phone out of my pocket. "Deva? What's going on?" She wouldn't call this late unless something was wrong. I couldn't help it, I started to pace as I waited for my mind to absorb what she was saying.

"The police were attacked. Beth was cornered and the... thing told her if she can't undo the spell by tomorrow night, it'll kill her. The thing left, but Beth is a mess, and we don't know what to do." She sounded really shaken. There was a waiver to her voice that I wasn't sure I'd ever heard before, which was saying something. My heart felt like it was being broken into a thousand pieces as my mind filled with images of what might have happened to Beth. If Daniel was this bad, then what chance did my friend stand?

"We're coming!" I cried. "Daniel is with me."

Daniel was already on his feet, his eyes that had been so soft a moment ago were hard as ice. "What?"

"Apparently the creature that attacked you attacked the police that were keeping an eye on Beth and cornered her. We have to undo the curse." My hand covered my mouth once the words had left my mouth, like I couldn't believe what I'd just said.

"Let's go." Daniel grabbed his keys from the table by my door where he'd laid them when he walked in. He held open the front door then closed it behind him. My hands shook as I tried to get my key in the lock, unwilling to leave Henry vulnerable. After they had scraped against the dead-bolt a couple of times Daniel gently took them from me and locked up.

As I rushed around to the passenger side of his truck, I couldn't help the sigh of relief at having someone like Daniel to go with me. He wasn't a witch, so he couldn't technically help with this, but it still felt good to have a partner in crime, so to speak. I wanted to get to Beth as quickly as possible, having to trust someone else to drive when I was already freaking out was hard, but if there was anyone who understood the severity of the situation, it was Daniel.

Now, I just hoped he could drive as fast as he moved.

## 18

**Emma**

AS WE CHANGED LANES, A CAR CAME OUT OF NOWHERE AND swerved in front of Daniel. He slammed on the brakes and cursed under his breath as the sports car sped down the highway. Glaring at the taillights of the fast little car, I wanted to give the bad driver an immediate Karmic punishment. But even though I didn't feel myself do it, apparently my new special ability did it for me. Seconds later, a police officer on a motorcycle pulled out from behind a small copse of trees and sped off after the bright red car.

"No way," Daniel whispered. He glanced at me and I saw suspicion on his face.

But I knew. Beaming, I wished it wasn't so dark so the driver could see the shit-eating grin on my face as we passed by him, pulled over and about to get a big, fat ticket from the police officer. "Nice," I muttered as we went on our way.

Sometimes being Karma was freaking awesome.

"You okay?" he asked, after a quiet minute.

I nodded. "This supernatural world is still just so new to me."

His one hand on the steering wheel seems to tighten. "Yeah, well, not many people learn about it in this stage of our lives. Although, I kind of think the world would be better off if all supernaturals didn't come into their powers until their forties."

"Why do you say that?" I asked, glad to have a distraction from my worries.

He shrugged. "Because we're all idiots when we're young. Giving teenagers the ability to shift, or use spells, or bite people, tends to bring a lot of trouble. I mean, I don't even want to think about my days as a young bear."

"I bet you were fine," I said, with a laugh.

He shook his head. "I once actually tried to get honey out of a beehive. I mean, I'd seen bears in movies do that all the time. It was not a smart decision, and my old man definitely gave me a talking to about reality versus how the media shows bears."

"How old were you when this happened?" I asked picturing a bear cub waddling around trying to get at honey.

"Old enough to know better," he replied with a chuckle.

I smiled, imagining Daniel as an awkward teenage bear covered in bee stings. "Well, I'd like to think my life would've been better. Instead of marrying a man who used me and threw me away..." I stopped talking, suddenly feeling ashamed of how I'd let my ex treat me for all those years. "But then again, I wouldn't have my son. And Travis was worth every hard moment of my marriage and my life. I guess there's some truth to the fact that we all end up where we're supposed to be."

"Agreed," Daniel said, a smile teasing his full lips. "And what's your son like?"

"Travis," I gushed his name. "That kid is incredible. I take credit for the sweet, intelligent, handsome man he's grown up to be. He's in college, pursuing his engineering degree. He treats women with respect. And he remembers to call his old mom just often enough that I still feel loved, even though he's in a stage of his life where he doesn't need me as much."

Daniel sighed. "I always wanted kids, but we just never could have them. I'd accepted that maybe that wasn't in the cards for me. Though, sometimes, I wish I'd had a son or daughter I could teach things to. You know, how to chop wood. How to make my mother's favorite stew. Stuff like that."

"Well, if you ever want to teach someone all that stuff, Travis will probably visit me sometimes, and that kid would drink up learning that kind of stuff. His dad never really paid him a lot of attention, so I've noticed he tends to gravitate to older men who have stories to tell." I smiled, even though Travis's lack of a real father-figure had always been a sore spot for me. "We had this older neighbor who liked to hunt and fish. Travis would trail after him any time he was working in his garage, and then he started taking him with him for short fishing days. Travis always came home grinning, like he'd never felt more special in his life."

Suddenly, it occurred to me that I'd just offered Daniel a semi-father role in my son's life. I felt my heart race and glanced over at him, fully expecting for him to have a *I need to get the hell out of here* look on his face.

Instead, he turned, and those stunning eyes of his seemed to twinkle. "I'd love that." Then, he cleared his throat. "So, does this mean you've officially decided to stay in Mystic Hollow?"

I laughed. "Well, nothing is official yet. I still need to wrap up my old life and deal with my ex."

Things were quiet for a long time, and we pulled into Carol's neighborhood. "About your ex," he began, then cleared his throat again, "what did he do after you left?"

I tried to hide my panic. Daniel didn't know about the whole toad thing. He was just making conversation. "Not really sure. But he's not really my problem anymore, thankfully. He and Candy are welcome to each other."

He said nothing more but seemed to accept my answer. Which made me relax a little, until I remembered why the hell we were driving in the middle of the night. It wasn't that I had forgotten. It was more than my nerves were so fried that I didn't even know how to manage the feeling of panic and worry inside of me.

Daniel pulled me up to the front door of Carol's house, where Beth was staying, as well as Deva. Carol's house had always looked so cheery, but right now, it was as if it radiated a sense of wrongness. The lights outside were all turned on bright, and a couple of police cars sat silent on the street. It almost felt like returning to an old neighborhood after the apocalypse. Everything was sort of the same, but different at the same time.

We climbed out of the truck and both rushed up the steps. With each second that passed, my heart hammered louder. Beth had escaped the thing, although with a warning. She was okay. I had to remember that. But even though everything I was thinking was logical, I felt sick as I pushed open the door and rushed inside.

"We're here!" Not wanting to scare them anymore than they already were.

Beth sat on the couch with Deva and Carol flanking her. All of them had tea in their hands, but set down the mugs when they saw us, glancing toward the police officers like they didn't know what to do. And all three of them looked pale and scared. Not that I blamed them.

Daniel crossed the room to the officers. Good, he could question them and find out what happened. I could find out what happened from the ladies' perspectives, and then we could piece together what happened and who did this.

Making a beeline for the couch, I said. "Are you guys okay?"

Deva nodded. "We're okay. Just a bit shaken up."

Carol scooted over on the couch so I could get close to Beth. "What happened?"

I sat down next to her and wrapped my hands around one of her hands. She was shaking, wearing a nightgown with little animals stitched onto the front, and a knitted robe over the top of it. Her long blonde hair, the hair that was always brushed perfectly straight, was a tangled mess around her face. And she didn't wear a drop of her beloved makeup, which told me she was really scared. Even when we were kids and had an emergency, Beth would be busy doing her makeup in the car.

"It's okay, Beth," Carol whispered, "just explain it one step at a time."

Beth shuddered and her skin felt damp and sweaty. "It was awful. It was Roger's old business partner, Cliff. Only, he was like this half wolf and half human thing." A tear rolled down her cheek. "And the look in his eyes... I was sure he was going to kill me. Like, I really thought I was going to die."

Damn it. The missing jerk was the one who was coming after Beth? No. Not a chance. His ass was going to pay.

"We're going to figure this out," I said, squeezing her

hand. "We won't let anything happen to you. Promise. Okay?"

Beth doesn't even seem to hear me. "I just can't get how unnatural he was out of my head. I just keep coming back to it. Whatever's powered this guy up, it's some dark magic."

Dark magic? Darn it. I didn't know anything about dark magic, but I guessed it was time to start figuring it out. If I didn't understand the difference between dark and light magic, how in the world was I going to help my friend?

"Did he tell you what he wanted?" Carol asked, giving me a look that said that this was the most Beth had spoken since the incident.

After a long minute, Beth nodded. "He seemed to think I was the one who did a spell on him. One he believed Roger had made me do. But I think he believed me when I told him I hadn't. That's when he threatened me and told me I have to figure out who cursed him and undo it."

"Who in the world could've helped Roger with a spell like that?" Deva asked as I rubbed Beth's hand with my thumbs.

"I don't know," Beth said, looking lost and alone.

"But we're going to figure it out," Deva said, and she looked furious, even in her flannel pjs.

"That's right," Carol nodded, wearing a shirt that said, "Knit Happens," with knitting needles under it. "And we're going to make them pay. Just focus on that."

Beth shuddered. "I'm sorry, I just can't stop thinking about how he looked. How he *felt*. He was so wrong. Like even the air around him knew that something like that wasn't supposed to exist."

Deva and I exchanged a look, then I pressed for the information we needed. "Do you have any idea who might have done that kind of spell for Roger?"

She sniffled, and a tear rolled down her cheek. "I don't know any other witch he might've been close to. I can't imagine who he would've gotten to do magic like that. I don't think I've ever met a witch that dark."

Damn it. That left us with nothing to go off. Except, heck, I really didn't want to do this.

Deva met my gaze, and I knew she was thinking the same thing I was. "We're going to have to talk to Tiffany."

I nodded. "I agree. And fast."

Carol made a little sound. "That cheating little traitor better have the information we need."

I lifted a brow.

She glared back at me. "What? I'm not always Miss Sunshine. Especially when I get woken up."

"She is so grumpy when you wake her up," Deva mumbled.

Carol shot her a dirty look. "I'm not that bad."

Deva crossed her arms over her chest. "Tell that to your cats, who happen to run and hide until you have your coffee."

To my relief, their banter made Beth smile. "Thanks, guys. I appreciate having bloodthirsty friends in a time like this."

"Always," I told her.

Now, to finally get some answers.

## 19

**Emma**

WE ALL STAYED THE NIGHT WITH CAROL. IT WAS LIKE SOME weird somber slumber party, where we were all grumpy and nervous out of our minds. We were even too tired for snacks and wine. And that was saying something because our little group loved our wine and snacks. Though, I wanted to meet the person that didn't love snacks and wine. Wait. Scratch that. I definitely didn't want to meet them because we were not on the same wavelength.

Daniel left late but not until I promised to call him before we tried anything. He'd helped wrap up some of the injuries on the officers and had stayed until after the police had gone home and two other police officers had taken up guard in their cars outside Carol's house. Then, lingered as if he wasn't sure he should go at all.

I'd smiled at him and said, "it's okay. We got this."

He'd still looked uncertain, so I'd put a hand on his arm and explained, "You're going to need to rest up. I have a feeling we'll need you tomorrow."

As soon as I stopped talking, I'd gotten the unmistakable impression he wanted to kiss me again, but then he'd simply patted my arm and headed out. Casting me a lingering glance before disappearing outside.

For some reason, I was glad he was such a gentleman, even if a part of me just wanted to jump on that hunk of a man after being sexually unfulfilled for so long with my ex. Yeah, I'd cave under those stunning eyes of Daniel's, but I wasn't ready for it yet, so I was thankful he always managed to hold back.

I bunked in with Beth, with Carol on her other side, in Carol's bed. It was a tight squeeze, but she needed the extra support, at least for the few hours of sleep we were able to get. Deva snored, so she got her room to herself.

The next morning, we got ready as best we could, then headed for Beth's sister's house across town. After a few snappy remarks to each other, we'd all agreed to stop for some coffee. Deva had made a comment about how angry witches and a long day were not a good combination. I agreed.

We'd pulled up outside of the same mall coffee shop where I liked to people watch and hurried out of the car toward the little shop, nearly crashing into two well-dressed sirens. For a minute, I thought one of them would shout at me. But the instant her eyes landed on me; she bowed her head. Then, elbowed the siren next to her, who also bowed her head.

"Great Karma, we have continued to fulfill our promise to the Great Mother. We have all been donating money to worthy charities. The queen has created a day each week where we fish the seas for garbage, and we are working on creating a preserve from some of our lands."

It was funny. When these ladies had tried to kill my

brother, they'd treated us like garbage. But since restoring their waters, I was like a goddess to them. "I'm glad you've kept your word."

The second lady looked up, her gaze meeting mine. "And already two of our women are pregnant."

I smiled, genuinely happy for them. "That's wonderful."

They both bowed again, then scurried out of the way.

"Oh, Great Karma, will you honor us by buying coffee together," Carol said, bursting into laughter.

I cast her a dark look. "Coffee first. Mocking me second."

"Very well," she said, stretching out the words so that she sounded like a ghost.

Deva shook her head swung the door open so we could all rush for the counter. We each gave our orders, and then, a few minutes later, we were back in our car. All of us just sat for a minute, inhaling the scents of our powerful brews. The only thing that would make this better would be some muffins or donuts or something that Deva had cooked up, only I knew she hadn't had time, so I'd have to be happy with my black gold.

"Now, this is magic," I sighed with contentment as the warm liquid trailed down my insides and pooled in my stomach.

Carol laughed. "The best kind! The kind that renews our spirits!"

I was starting to feel a little more chipper as I sipped my French Vanilla latte when Beth finally spoke. "It's going to be weird to see Tiffany."

I stiffened and looked at the others. Beth always told me about how hard it was living in town with her ex, and seeing her little sister with him, on the phone. But what she told me, and what these ladies probably experienced with her daily was different. I honestly had no idea what to say.

"Why is that?" Deva asked gently.

Beth shrugged, staring at her coffee like it had the answers. "I've honestly tried not to wish harm on my sister and Roger over the years, but I've definitely had some nasty thoughts about them."

"Anyone would," I reassured her.

"But now, he's dead, and I can't be mad at him anymore. I know my sister is probably grieving right now, and I should find empathy inside of me to be kind to her... but I just... I don't know. I still feel so angry with them both."

"Unpopular opinion here," Deva began, "but we don't have to suddenly pretend like someone was a good person, just because they died. You go on hating Roger as much as you want! And it's okay to hate your sister, too. She didn't care when she hurt you."

Carol winced and turned to face Beth. "All that is true. But also, keep in mind that hating someone else is like poisoning yourself to poison your neighbor. While neither of them deserves your forgiveness, you deserve to not have that hate in your life anymore."

I nodded, seeing wisdom in what both of them said. "Just remember, however you feel today, that's okay. We won't think any less of you. You're allowed to feel whatever you feel."

"Thanks, guys," she said, looking relieved.

Deva fired up the car, and we headed through town toward an area known as the rich part of town. No, these neighborhoods didn't line the beach, but they were massive, more along the lines of small mansions than anything else. As kids, we'd drive through these neighborhoods picking out the houses we wanted to live in one day. When Beth and Roger had bought a house here, it was like all Beth's dreams were coming true. She'd spent weeks and months fixing it up exactly the way she thought they'd both enjoy. As an adult, I wouldn't trade my beach house for any of the houses on this side of town.

Carol had told me that Beth hadn't taken a single thing from the house when she'd left. Just her clothes, photo albums, that kind of stuff. She'd left every piece of furniture, every painting, everything that she'd selected with such love and care. That was, I guess, the only good thing about my ex. His new girlfriend hadn't wanted to live in my "dumpy" house, so he'd left me there.

Even though he later planned to take it from me, probably to sell and buy something "better."

Damn. Exes could be brutal.

We ended up slipping behind another car as the gates opened into Beth's old neighborhood. Slowly, we drove past the expansive estates, with their perfectly trimmed lawns, and their perfectly painted houses. All of us were silent, trying to casually glance at Beth to see how she was feeling. When we at last pulled up to her old house, the white and pink building reminded me of the White House with all it's perfectly lined up windows and giant, oversized pillars out front. It sat there looking regal but also a little run down and overgrown.

"I can't believe I used to live here with Roger," Beth said bitterly. "And now my sister lives here."

I couldn't imagine that feeling. Actually, I could. When I'd seen my ex's new girl wearing my mother's locket, I'd been enraged. And turned them both into toads. I bet Beth wished she'd been able to do the same all those years ago.

"It's okay," I said soothingly. "She'll get hers." Hey, I was Karma. I knew it was true.

And if it didn't happen on its own, I could always *help*.

Beth sucked in a deep breath and opened her car door.

We all marched out, and Deva handed around tiny sugar cookies, for courage, she said. Where she'd been hiding those when I'd started drinking my coffee earlier, I didn't know, but I kind of wished I'd had them then and not now. That being said I was happier to have them than not. I wasn't sure if they were actually magicked, but the second the sweet treat hit my mouth, I felt a lot better. Slamming the remains of my coffee, and only getting a few drops from the cup, I shoved the empty container in the little cup holder, then turned to face the house.

"How do you want to handle this, boss?" I asked Beth.

She put her small shoulders back. "Head on."

As she hurried across the lawn, she passed a little gnome. Freezing, she pointed at it. "I picked that out. Someone throw it in the trunk."

I was half surprised that gnomes weren't real beings in the supernatural world, but Carol grinned, snatched it up without an ounce of hesitation, and headed for the trunk.

As Beth passed a little glass heart partially hidden in a bush, she froze, turned, and kicked it. The glass went flying as it shattered, and a triumphant smile touched her lips. "You know, the twins were at school when they told me they'd been having an affair and wanted me out. All I'd done was cry and pack up. I'd spent hours dragging what I could of the kids' stuff too and loading up my car, before luckily finding a house for rent from a friend's parents from high school. I'd been so focused on my broken heart; I hadn't even gotten angry. And then, afterward, I'd had to play nice for the kids. Now though? Now I don't have to play nice."

For some reason, I felt like this was an important moment for Beth. A moment that was long in coming. A time for her to stand up for herself.

Carol was back without the gnome. She gave a nod and dusted off her hands. "Let's go."

Beth marched up the porch steps, then rapped on the door firmly.

It didn't take long for her sister to answer.

Tiffany was wearing a white bikini and a white see-through covering over her shoulders. She wore ridiculously tall high heels, and her face and hair were done to the nines. She'd obviously braided her hair in an intricate design, like something off an online hair tutorial video. And, as much as I felt like a jerk, she didn't look anything like a grieving widow.

In her hand was a martini glass with two olives, which she swung toward us, sloshing the vodka on the floor before saying, "Oh, it's you guys."

"Yeah," Beth said, tilting her chin up. "It is."

After an awkward second, she said, "Come in."

We walked in, through a foyer with a massively tall ceiling with a crystal chandelier. On the floor, in tile, were Roger's initials. She led us through that room to an open living room, that looked out on a massive pool and a rigid-looking garden. Tiffany sat gingerly on the sofa as Beth's face reddened.

"Is this the same furniture?" I whispered as quietly as I could do to Deva.

She arched one eyebrow. "Mmhmm."

Wow. As I glanced around, I realized that it was all the same furniture that Beth had picked out. In fact, the only thing that seemed to have been changed was that all the pictures were swapped out for ones with Tiffany and Roger. Hell, I was willing to bet they'd even used the same silver frames since they looked more to Beth's tastes than Tiffany's.

Hers would probably be sparkly or nonexistent, similar to her bikini.

Man, if Beth wasn't pissed before, she should be pissed now. It honestly felt like Roger had swapped her out for a younger version. Except that Tiffany lacked all useful skills, including design skills, so they'd just kept living in the beautiful space Beth had made.

It was awful. And, quite frankly, creepy.

"So," Beth said stiffly. The tension in the room was palpable. I wanted to burst into song or something to break it. "Here's what we know. Someone Roger was associated with put a curse on Cliff, Roger's ex-business partner. Now, Cliff thought it was me that did the curse, but I didn't know anything about it. There's no way I could handle the kind of magic that had to be done for this curse."

Tiffany looked at us with wide eyes. "Well, I didn't do it. You know I didn't get magic like you did."

Yeah, that was something to be grateful for. I couldn't imagine someone with her lack of an ethical code being given powers. She'd, no doubt, become some kind of fairy tale princess' villain.

"We thought you might know who it is." I gave Tiffany a firm look when she wouldn't meet my gaze. "Tiffany," I said with a warning in my tone. "You know something."

She shook her head. "I don't."

Carol sighed. "Do you know who Emma here is?"

Tiffany looked at me with wide, worried eyes. "No?"

"She's Karma." Deva grinned. "Literally. She can pay you back for every stupid, thoughtless, mean thing you've ever done in your life and all she has to do is *think* about it and that'll be you, screwed."

Tiffany gulped. "Here's the thing. Uh. You know he cheated on you with me, but I wasn't the only one," she whispered. "I knew about the other woman, and when he and I started our life together—"

Beth scoffed and glared at her sister. "There's no way he was cheating before he met you."

Her sister wouldn't meet her gaze. "I caught her with him when I was in high school. But you know how he bought me a new car when I turned seventeen? It was actually because I threatened to tell you if he didn't."

Beth looked like she'd been physically struck. "You betrayed me for a car?"

"A really nice car," she rushed out. "And I would've eventually told you, but then, I didn't see them together again, so I just kind of forgot about it."

"Freaking convenient," Deva muttered angrily.

Tiffany flinched. "I know. But when we eventually started dating, I told him he had to break it off with her or I wouldn't keep sleeping with him. As far as I know, he did."

Gosh. I hated everything about this woman.

"So, what does she have to do with anything?" Deva asked in a sassy tone of voice.

"She was a witch," Tiffany said, as if it was obvious. "A powerful witch, supposedly."

"More," Carol growled. "You know more."

Tiffany scuffed her toe on the carpet, digging it in as though she could dig herself out of this situation. "Um, her name was Catrin. As far as I heard, he hired her to turn Cliff into some animal or another. Then, Roger took over the business."

Man, this woman and Roger really were the perfect match. Two cheating scumbags who would stop at nothing to screw over everyone around them.

I could feel my body tingling. No, I hadn't consciously

called on my powers, but karma was having trouble holding back.

"I doubt she would kill him though," Tiffany rushed out. "If she wanted to, she would've done it a long time ago."

"No, she isn't trying to kill him, but Cliff is, because now the spell is falling apart." Beth sighed and rubbed her eyes. "And Cliff is coming for us all."

Tiffany went pale and drained the rest of her martini from the glass, before fishing out the olives and chewing on them like crazy. But call me heartless, I didn't feel even a little bad for her.

"Where do we find this witch, Catrin?" I asked wearily. It was going to suck going after this one.

With a sigh, Tiffany wrote down an address. "Don't tell her you got this from me, please. I have no way to fight back against her."

I scoffed at Beth's little sister. "You'd deserve it if we did."

Her eyes widened.

Beth spoke before I could. "But we won't."

As we all stood, the others headed for the door, but I lingered back with Tiffany. When her gaze met mine, I said. "Karma should have punished you a long time ago, but she will now."

"No," she squeaked.

"Whatever the universe decides is your punishment."

"What if I play nice with Beth again?" she rushed out, then pointed to the sofa. "She could have some of the furniture."

I smiled but it wasn't a nice one, and she stepped away from me, looking nervous. "No, you stay away from Beth. Be alone forever, like you deserve."

And even though my words weren't a spell, they felt like one. Yeah, Karma could hit her with a bus. Karma could make all her hair fall out and make her butt the size of a couch. But spending her life alone? That was what she truly deserved.

And when we spoke to the witch and were done dealing with Cliff, Beth would have the happiness she deserved. I swore it.

## 20

## Emma

"Are we ready for this?" Deva asked. "I made a few hex bags, but I'd rather not use them on a witch like this."

"I'll do what I can," I muttered. "Maybe my powers will really kick in and help." I honestly wasn't sure that they would. Sometimes it seemed like the more I tried to reach for them the further out of my grasp they went. I was trying to grab onto smoke. And sometimes, they worked when I least expected them too.

As much as I knew my power had to be instinctual on some level, I also wanted control. There was too much in my life that was out of control, I couldn't stand it if my powers were the same and just burst out of me whenever they wanted. Sure, I'd made the waterfall flow, I'd even made that bully of a big brother run into his mom, but any time I tried to get Karma to do its job, it was hard, like walking on a sprained ankle, hard. When I'd first tried, I'd say it was more like walking on a broken ankle though, so at least it was getting better. I sent a silent prayer to whoever might be listening that I could do what I needed to in order to protect my friend.

Beth looked at the small house with fear in her eyes. "We have to. If she's as dark as it seems we won't have a choice." The house was severe, all squares, metal and glass. Were those shipping containers? The closer we got to it the more I realized they had to be, there was nothing else that looked like that. The corrugated metal was a deep blue, and one end of a container still had the stickers and labeling on it. No joke. There was some siding around the rectangle that made up the front door area, as well as a little awning over the front steps. That was about the only normal part though. Everything else was either shipping container or window. It felt oddly exposed seeing floor to ceiling windows on a house like that if it could even be called a house. The windows allowed us to see inside though, and it was remarkable, from the inside I wouldn't have guessed that the place was made of containers like that. It looked like a totally normal house.

Throwing open the passenger door, I stepped out of the car to get the ball rolling. If one of us didn't move, then we would stay there waiting for hours as we worked up the courage to face this dark witch. It helped that I didn't quite know what that meant. I was blissful in my ignorance of the different types of magic.

As soon as everyone was out of the car, I strode forward and rapped on the door. We had to get this figured out, had to save Beth. We didn't have much time.

A woman opened the door with a knowing look on her face. As her gaze flitted from me, to Carol, to Deva. She smiled smugly, but then when she saw Beth, her smile broke into a wide grin. "Well, well, well." She clearly knew exactly who we were and part of me hoped she knew why we were here as well. It would certainly make things easier if we didn't have to catch her up on everything.

"Catrin?" I asked, needing to be sure before we launched any kind of attack at this woman. She looked unassuming, her mousy brown hair was pulled back in a French braid, and her eyes were framed with large, square rimmed glasses that had to be some kind of tortoise shell pattern. Behind the lenses sat eyes that were such a deep brown they almost looked black. They seemed to dance with amusement at the situation and also seemed more than a little observant. Anyone might overlook this woman without a second thought, but that would be a mistake on their part. At least if she was the dark witch we were looking for.

She kept grinning and nodded once. "That's me." She popped her hip to the side and tilted her head slightly as though she was trying to figure out what was going on.

"Can we come in?" I asked in a sarcastic voice, but I didn't give her time to answer. I just pushed forward. "Great, thanks."

The inside of the weird shipping containers was about as normal as a home could get. There was nothing in it that screamed "I'm an evil witch who likes to destroy relationships." Cream colored walls met hardwood flooring, or at least what looked like hardwood floors. A black leather sofa was about the evillest looking thing in there, and that wasn't even so much about the color as the fact that it looked uncomfortable as all hell. The living area led back into a kitchen and beyond that I could see stairs leading to the container that was on top of this one, and what I thought was a bathroom as well. In every corner of the place there were plants, everything from ferns to succulents to orchids.

If I didn't know she was a dark witch, I would have assumed she was an earth witch or something similar.

Catrin walked regally in front of me, indicating I should stay in the living area, but I wanted to put her off her game, so I moved past her walking into the kitchen, which was a challenge since the place was so narrow. I propped myself up at the end of her countertop where there were a couple bar stools. "This will do," I said with my nose in the air. "We're here to discuss the curse on Cliff."

As everyone moved to take seats around the area, Catrin's smile grew more Cheshire-like. "Oh?"

"Stop acting so coy," Beth said in a low, dangerous voice.

Catrin's smile took on a cold edge, like she was an animal showing her teeth instead of a woman smiling. "I am anything but coy."

With a sigh, I decided to hurry this along. "I'm guessing that you've done some pretty terrible things in your life, Catrin."

Her gaze snapped to me. "And that means?"

Deva leaned back in her chair. "You're a mercenary, aren't you? A magical mercenary."

For the first time, Catrin's smile disappeared. "That's a pretty big charge."

Magical mercenary? They hadn't called her that before. What did that even mean? Could anyone suffer at her hands? Were all the rules that seemed to bind the rest of the magical community off the table?

"The thing is, Catrin, the thing is..." I paused and let her stew for a moment before I said, "You don't realize who I am." I smiled at her encouragingly. "Go on. Ask."

The dark witch rolled her eyes, not picking up on the happy warning I was trying to give her. In many ways even though she was a grown woman she came off as a teenager.

Like she'd never completely matured into who she was supposed to be. "And who are you supposed to be, as if I care?"

Carol leaned forward. "Allow me to introduce you to the one, the only... Karma."

As we let the words sink in, I turned slightly so I could focus on her refrigerator. Apparently Catrin had done some terrible things, because with a pop, smoke began to rise from the back of it. "Oh, no," I said in a sing-song voice. "Looks like your fridge just went on the fritz."

Catrin whirled around taking in the fact that her fancy stainless steel, top of the line, fridge was now about as useful as a foam cooler, then looked at me with a healthy dose of suspicion in her eyes. "How?"

"Karma," Deva whispered.

I glanced at Beth, glad to see she looked a lot more confident with a sly look in her sky-blue eyes.

"Now, how about you tell us about this curse?" I spoke.

With a sniff, Catrin shrugged. "Easily fixed," she muttered.

I spotted her coffee pot, half full still. Focusing on it, I grinned when the carafe broke into a hundred tiny pieces of glass and the coffee splashed all over the counter. "Not quite as easily fixed," I whispered as I focused again until smoke rose from the motor of that appliance as well. "Oh, too bad."

When my gaze flicked to the microwave Catrin's face slowly darkened. "Stop."

"Speak," Deva retorted.

She still hesitated though, so I let my karmic powers roam, knowing that my instincts would find something that meant a lot to her. I heard a pop from upstairs. Catrin jumped up and booked it up the tiny staircase. When she came back down her face was thunderous. "My TV is cracked down the middle," she said in a low voice.

I focused more, reaching for the smoke that was my power, but this time instead of trying to grab it I mentally blew on it, encouraging it like you would the embers of a fire. Water began to spew from the faucet. Then, the small countertop dishwasher made a groaning sound before another loud pop made Catrin jump as water sprayed from it, before the door burst open and everything that had been inside seemed to shatter as water and shards of glass and china ran out. "Stop!" she cried.

"And why should I?" I asked.

"I'll help you. What do you want to know about the curse?" The desperation in her voice made me smile. Just like her, I showed too many teeth. The threat evident on my face. Her gaze flicked between the four of us, trying to figure out who was going to ask the next question. Like it needed to happen before something else broke.

"How do we stop it?" Beth asked as she slammed her hand down on the table in a surprising display of frustration. "If we don't reverse it, Cliff is going to kill me. And if you think your karma is bad now, think about how bad it'll be if that happens."

"We need to do it in that ugly office house thing of theirs," Catrin said in a voice that indicated that she'd really given up. Her shoulders slumped and she sighed. "It'll work better there. I turned Cliff into a wolf there. But I need some time to gather the ingredients. Meet me there at dusk." Her defeat was undoubtable, but in all the movies I'd watched and books I'd read, the dark witch was always crafty. They always had something else tucked up their sleeve. Or a go bag.

I stood and walked over to her. "If you don't meet us,

*nothing* will be able to hide you from Karma. I am every-where." I wasn't. Not really. But she didn't know that.

Her face which had been red with anger and shame a moment ago paled and her eyes widened. "I'll be there," she whispered.

## 21

**Emma**

"I can't believe she came," Beth said. We sat on the steps of Roger's office, waiting for Catrin. It was a half-hour after dark and we really didn't like being out here, but we'd gone inside, and it had felt ominous and uncomfortable. I couldn't help but remember the reaction of the ghosts the last time I was in there. Thus, the four of us were huddled on the concrete steps outside the front door to the office.

Catrin had pulled up a few seconds ago. She got out, carrying a black bag that appeared to be loaded down with stuff. What on earth she needed that much stuff for I wasn't sure, but it made my stomach twist with dread. She'd dressed for the occasion in all black.

Her skinny jeans were more than just skinny, they were skintight and had holes in the knees and thighs, while her black t-shirt had the name of a band I didn't recognize plastered across the front, and she topped the outfit off with a long black duster cardigan. A large silver pendant gleamed at the base of her throat, drawing the eye. Oh, and don't

forget the black combat boots, or maybe they were Doc
Martens, it was hard to tell in the dark, though Doc Martens
seemed like they were probably too old for her, or not cool
enough. Either way they were heeled and ankle height,
and... was that an honest to goodness witch's hat hooked to
the side of the duffle bag? Was there a reason to have a
witch's hat? Surely, they didn't have to wear one when practicing magic, I mean I'd never seen any of my friends in one.
What other reason could it have though?

"Okay," she called as she walked across the gravel of the
parking area. "Let's do this." She pushed her glasses up on
her nose as she came closer, studying me warily. Part of me
wondered if she'd done some checking after we'd left earlier
and found out that Karma was real and inhabited a person.
Whatever had happened, I was glad for the change in her
demeanor. If she hadn't stopped with the snarky teenager
routine, even though she was at least in her late twenties, I
would have had to smack her upside the head. Someone
would have needed to teach her some respect.

We stood as a group and as I was about to turn and open
the door something... huge... appeared out of nowhere. This
thing towered over us and was walking on two legs, but they
were distorted, backward almost. Large arms hung loosely
at its sides and it had hands with claws that were more like
blades at the end of each fingertip, each one curving
outward and ending in a vicious looking point.

Black fur covered most of its body, which I was grateful
for as it also appeared to be naked, and it was only when I
looked at its head that I realized this must be Cliff. His face
was distorted as though he was stuck halfway between
changing from a wolf to a man or vice versa. He had an
elongated jaw, but it wasn't full canine, more like an incred-

ibly severe underbite, and the slope of his face made it look like his eyes should be sitting further back than they were.

"No," I cried. Whirling, I tried to yank the door open, but it had automatically relocked after a certain period and I knew Beth wouldn't be able to get it open again before he attacked us.

Cliff lunged forward, coming after Beth. She darted across the parking lot and around our car, her eyes wide with fear as she tried to keep something between herself and Cliff. He paced toward her, unhurried in his attack, as though he already knew the outcome and it was inevitable.

And I swear, in that moment. I felt like her fate was sealed.

## 22

**Emma**

"Hex bags!" Carol screamed.

My hands trembled as I reached inside my pocket, and I threw the bag. It hit the side of the thing's head, and he whirled toward me and hissed. Smoke and sparks flew all over his face for a minute, and he snarled and smacked himself, trying to put the sparks out.

"Ignis!" Deva shouted and threw her bag at his feet.

His feet caught fire, and he howled in rage, then began to roll to try to put himself out. He was successful, far too quickly.

Carol shouted. "Glutinum!"

Suddenly, a sticky substance covered the creature. He tried to stand, but he couldn't.

"Yes!" I shouted.

Beth inched closer from around the side of the car.

And then, he shoved himself up, and we heard his fur tearing from the ground. "Death," he growled, then launched toward Beth.

My heart stopped. I put my hand out, trying to use my powers, but nothing happened.

*Calm down.* I commanded myself. *Calm down and just focus!*

But still, nothing happened.

Carol and Deva threw more hex bags, shouting spells, the beast leaped over the car and onto Beth, knocking her to the ground. We all ran in a panic to see him crushed on top of her, his claws drawn back, ready to strike.

"Stop!" Deva screamed, another hex bag already in her hand that she'd yet to throw. "We're trying to undo the spell!"

To my surprise, Cliff paused, panting, he tilted his head as though considering Deva's words. I was honestly shocked he could understand and that the wolf brain hadn't taken over completely. If it did part of me wondered if we would sound like Charlie Brown's teachers to him. When he swung his head around to face Deva, I had to fight my instinct to run to her, if I did it might set him off even further and it seemed like he had a hair-trigger to begin with.

"Explain," he said in a growly voice that sounded mostly animalistic.

It didn't seem like Cliff had noticed Catrin yet, who stood frozen. Her face had gone even paler than it had in her home when I threatened her. Her eyes were as round as the witch's saucers as she took in Cliff's form. Hadn't she done this? Why did she look so surprised? And so scared?

"She brought what we need to reverse the spell. We can fix this," Carol said in a loud voice. We instinctively tried to spread out, knowing that the more we did, the more he would have to circle to keep his attention on all of us.

"We're trying to help you," I said, so he had to whirl around once more, and those strange eyes looking out from an almost human face were focused on me. I swallowed roughly as I tried to think of what else I could say to keep his attention off Beth.

It turned out I didn't need to say anything because Catrin's boot scuffed against the gravel as she took a step backward. I swore if she ran, I'd just let him have at her. Cliff's head swung toward the sound and his gaze landed on Catrin. I knew in that instant that he recognized her. The very air around us seemed to drop in temperature until I felt like I was standing somewhere in the Arctic Circle. A low, constant rumble seemed to leak from his chest as he growled, "You... You did this, didn't you?"

Catrin squeaked and held out the bag. "I'm here to undo it." The sassy, smug, know-it-all witch from earlier was nowhere to be seen on her terrified features.

Cliff's rage overtook him at her words. In a split second, he was off Beth and running on paws and hands, he galloped toward her before any of us could properly react, moving more like a gorilla than a human or wolf. Lashing out with one hand, those wicked-looking claws extended toward his target, he slashed Catrin across the throat.

"No," I whispered as her head flopped backward. Blood sprayed forth, covering him. He'd almost cut through her neck completely, almost beheaded her, and the only reason her head hung on was with some muscles and skin behind her spine, which he hadn't severed. Nausea rolled through me at the sight. I'd never expected something like that.

Growling and howling in turn, Cliff turned back to Beth. "It's not over," he growled.

As he lunged for her, I finally reacted and focused all the Karmic power I could muster on him. I drew the smoke of my power into my lungs, breathing it in, letting it suffuse my entire being before I began shouting nonsense. I tensed every muscle in my body as my power blasted into him. I willed the smoke forth, trying to visualize it forming a cloud around him until he was choking on it and couldn't breathe without inhaling the karma that was owed to him.

All the bad things he'd done while alive mixed with my power and dosed him everything he deserved. He couldn't escape it, couldn't run from it, though he tried, as I watched him stumble about.

A moment later the air around him seemed to shimmer and in the place of the half-wolf, half-man, all monstrous creature that he had been there was instead a small, gray rat that flopped to the ground and squeaked. Its little nose twitched, and his whiskers seemed to shiver for a second before it sneezed. I partly expected him to turn back into the wolf-man creature, but he didn't. The rat just sat there shaking his head in confusion. Or maybe he needed to sneeze again. Who could say?

Thinking fast, Deva grabbed her purse and dumped its contents on the ground before running over to Cliff and scooping him up in the gray leather bag, then quickly zipping it up before he could fight back. The outraged squeaking filled the night air. The only sound to be heard.

We all stared at each other, chests heaving, then almost in unison our gazes turned to the body of Catrin, bleeding out on the asphalt. As soon as the claws had sliced through her neck, I knew there had been no way to save her. A wound like that? Not a chance in hell. Seeing her body lying there, the blood pooling around her was more than I could stand though, and I had to turn away.

Sure, she'd been a magical mercenary, but she was young, she could have turned her life around. Maybe this would have been the kick in the pants she needed to get on the right track. Now we'd never know though. She was a casualty of her own curse, but one I hadn't wanted.

"Now what?" Beth whispered.

## 23

**Emma**

THE POLICE FINISHED THEIR QUESTIONING AS WE ALL SAT together on the sidewalk of Roger's building. A quiet ambulance took the dark witch away, although there were no sirens, and no lights. There was no reason to rush off when the person was already dead. We gathered as close to Beth as we could to offer her our silent support, but I could see it in her eyes. Maybe this wasn't how she wanted things with her ex to end, but she was glad there was an ending, at last.

The sheriff closed the book he'd been taking notes in and looked away from his deputy toward us. Very slowly, he headed our way. When he reached us, to my surprise, he removed his hat and crouched down in front of Beth.

"Well, everything seems to be as you said it was," he said, speaking gentler than he had when he was questioning us. He nodded toward the purse that held Cliff the rat. "You got a plan for him?"

"Yeah," Deva told him firmly, "we have a plan."

He nodded again and stared down at his hat. "Beth, you

know everyone in town had your back with all that disgusting nonsense with your sister and your ex. I just wanted you to know that we're still here for you. And us, in the force, are grateful for your business. You've helped a lot of people with all this supernatural crap. When we can't help, it's good to know that we have someone like you who can. Never underestimate yourself and how much we appreciate you."

Beth drew herself up a little taller. "Thank you."

The sheriff seemed like he wanted to say more. He looked at me a couple times, then eventually stood up to his full height with a slight groan. "You ladies need any of us to give you a ride home?"

Carol shook her head. "We're okay. We've actually gotten pretty good at taking care of each other."

"I've noticed that," he said with a smile.

He turned back, and he and the deputy got back in their car. The sheriff gave a wave out his window before he took off, and then we were left together in the quiet parking lot.

"So, it's really over?" Beth asked.

I took her hand and squeezed it. "I think it is."

Carol grinned and leaped to her feet. "No more creepy stalkers! No more death threats! No more weird notes! And, finally, a good night's rest. Absolutely do not call me before noon tomorrow, because I plan to sleep like the dead."

"Don't say that," Deva said with a wince.

We all laughed.

Then, they looked back at me. "You should bring Daniel the rat."

I'd been a little surprised no one had called him. I'd been tempted to, but it sort of felt like this case was open and shut. There was no real need to wake the bear shifter late at night, except that I wanted to see him.

"Okay." I tried not to seem too pleased about having to see Daniel. "I'll take care of it."

"There's one thing though…" Beth began, then stopped.

"What is it?" I coaxed.

"I know we're still learning about Karma, but I'm not sure if your ex and his girlfriend will remain toads forever."

My heart raced. "Why?"

She shook her head. "I don't know. That doesn't seem to be how karma works. Right?"

I thought about it. No, karma only really punished people the way they needed to be punished.

"If they learn their lessons," Carol began slowly, as if she was thinking, "could they possibly turn back into humans?"

I felt sick. "I think it's possible."

"We may want to plan a trip back there," Deva told me gently. "This seems like the kind of situation we should take care of before it becomes something worse."

As much as I didn't want to think about all this right now, they had a point. Besides, my ex being a toad didn't feel like the end of my story with him. I wanted to fully close the chapter like Beth had, even though I didn't need Rick to die or anything.

"Let's plan for it." Then, I looked at Deva, suddenly remembering a conversation we'd had before. "And have you fully closed the door with Harry?"

She suddenly looked very serious. "This whole thing has made me realize that life is far too short. First thing tomorrow, I'm telling him there is no chance we'll ever get back together. And then, I might go visit a certain handsome doctor and see if he'll ask me out."

"Or you could ask him out?" Carol said, eyes twinkling.

Deva grinned. "Yeah, I might just do that."

We all stood and headed for the car. Deva carried the rat

in her purse, and I knew they'd have to drop me off to get my car and then go to Daniel's house. As tired as I was, just the thought of visiting him put a little spring in my step.

"So, all the people who stirred up this trouble are gone now," Carol sounded amused. "Karma really does seem to know how to execute justice on the corrupt. Maybe you should tell karma to help out your friends too."

I wiggled my fingers at her, not really planning to use magic, but I still felt a strange tingle move down my spine. "As you wish!"

She laughed and shook her head; I was only joking.

We were about to climb into the car when a dark car moved past. It got caught at the light, and I think we all turned to see who was still up in our sleepy town at this hour. The dark windows on the car were all rolled down, and a man turned to look at us. He had dark hair and a chiseled jaw, but when his gaze fell on us, his eyes widened. The light turned green, and he sped off.

"Who was that?" I asked.

No one answered, so I turned to face them. Carol had gone absolutely sheet white.

"Guys?" I prodded, looking at Deva and Beth.

Beth nibbled her bottom lip. "It probably wasn't him. It's been a long time. And it was dark."

"Him who?" I pressed.

Carol spoke, her tone far too level. "It looked like Bryan. But after disappearing on me all those years ago, I know he'd never have the guts to show his face here again."

"But--"

"It wasn't him." She opened her car door and slammed it shut.

My gaze met Deva's. "It's been a long night. Let's just forget about it," she said.

But if it was him, I was sure this wasn't done yet.

They drove me home while an old song we all loved played. At first it was just Beth who sang along, but by the time we reached my house, we were all belting out the words. When the song ended, we all grinned at each other, and awkward hugs were exchanged in the car.

"I'm glad I came back," I told them.

"We are too," Deva said. "Now, do you know if it's going to be permanent?"

I smiled. "Yeah, I just have to wrap up a few things back home."

"Well, we're here to help you wrap them up," Beth said with a laugh.

I got out of my car, and Deva pulled a metal trash can out of the trunk, and we threw the little rat in that too. They watched as I climbed into my car, and then I headed to Daniel's house. I spent the entire drive smiling. Beth was safe. The creepy creature was caught, and currently, a rat.

Life was good.

And, I had a feeling, it would only get better. Once I saw Daniel...

## 24

**Emma**

I HAD MY BRIGHTS ON AS I WENT DOWN THE LITTLE DIRT ROAD that led to Daniel's cabin. To my surprise, I liked the dark woods around me and the quiet of knowing I wouldn't be running into anyone else on this road. Whatever reason Daniel had chosen to live out here, probably bear-related, was smart. I'd love to live in a place like this.

When I pulled up outside of the cabin, I turned my lights off and just sat for a moment. His cabin looked so dang picturesque. I wished instead of me being here to bring him a rat, I was pulling up to a place that was mine too. Boy, that thought would probably freak him out. But I could almost picture us sitting together inside, drinking cocoa before a fire.

His door flew open, and he stood, silhouetted by what must have been a warm fire inside. He was wearing a white t-shirt and long pajama pants. Seeing the outfit on anyone else, I might have laughed. But he was all man in his clothes. So much so that my mouth went dry.

I killed the engine and opened my door as he came out toward me. "What's going on?" he called, and I instantly felt bad about not calling him and warning him that I was coming.

"Everyone is okay," I told him instantly and unbuckled.

"Then," he hesitated. "Uh, is this a social call?"

I felt my cheeks heat. "No, I brought something for you."

He lifted a brow. "A gift?"

"Not exactly." I peered down into the metal garbage can in the seat beside me. "Well, Rat-Cliff, your time is up." Grabbing the garbage can, I stepped out of the car. "This whole mess is over. The curse is broken, so to speak."

Daniel seemed confused. "Come in and explain, please. And what's with the trash can?"

I laughed uneasily. "Your gift. Well, not a gift. If this was a present, it would be the worst present ever."

He gave me a funny look, but headed back up the porch, and held his front door open for me. I followed him inside, feeling confident until the door closed behind me, and I realized we were alone in pretty much the coziest cabin I had ever seen. This seemed like the kind of place you went to for a romantic getaway, not to deliver a man-rat to a potential love interest. It was also pleasantly warm inside with a cheery fire crackling away. But that was the only sound. A thick, hardback book rested in the seat of a recliner near the fire. Daniel had been reading.

I loved that. A man who liked to read. A rare commodity anymore. "I'm sorry to bother you."

"No." He took the trash can from me and motioned toward the couch. "You've made my night infinitely better by coming." But then, he peered down into the can. "Um, what's this?"

"That," I said carefully, "is Cliff, Roger's ex-business

partner who has been missing for five years." I plopped down on the couch and sighed, happy to be able to relax after such an exhausting day.

"Wh..." Daniel gave me a cockeyed glance. "What?"

"Set him down. He's not climbing out of that. He almost chewed through the purse we had him in, so we had to find something he couldn't get himself out of."

Daniel nodded and put the can on the coffee table, then sat beside me. "Start at the beginning."

"Okay, so we tracked the curse to a witch named Catrin who Roger had an affair with when he was married to Beth. I had to lean on Catrin a little, but in the end, I was able to get her to admit that she'd cursed Cliff." I sighed and told the rest. "And when we went to the office to undo the spell, Cliff turned up. He, ah, he killed the witch, Catrin before we could even think about fighting back."

A wave of sadness came over me. I'd help run a business for years. I wasn't a soldier or a police officer. It wasn't a part of my daily life to see people die. I didn't think I'd ever forget watching that witch be attacked like that. It was sad, even if she had a responsibility in all of this.

"What did you do after that?" Daniel asked, his tone gentle.

He must have realized that it was a traumatic thing to see someone die, even if that someone used dark magic, cheated, and overall seemed to be a terrible person. I was glad I didn't have to explain the way I felt to him.

I released a slow breath. "By the time he turned to attack Beth, I had time to gather my thoughts and my magic and..." I motioned to the trash can. "I unleashed Karma on him."

"Karma?" He lifted a brow.

I nodded. "That's who, or what, I am now, Daniel. That's why I suddenly have powers. I'm Karma."

His brows drew together, and he was quiet for a long minute before he said, "Okay."

"Just okay?" I asked, studying him carefully.

I kind of expected him to be shocked. Or ask a lot of questions. His quiet acceptance of something I was still struggling to accept felt weird.

"Well," he gave a small smile. "You kind of accepted the whole bear shifter thing pretty easily."

I couldn't help but return his smile. "Well, I've always kind of liked bears. And, somehow, the whole thing fits you. It feels like I can't like you without..." I realized what I was saying but caught myself. "I can't accept Daniel without accepting you're a bear. So, I did."

He rubbed the back of his neck, looking pleased. "So, you unleashed... karma on the guy."

"Yup," I gestured to the trash can. We both leaned forward and looked down at the brown tear-drop shaped creature. Its claws scraped against the bottom of the trash can as though it was trying to dig itself out, but there was no chance he was going to get through the metal. Every so often he'd stop as though he needed to catch his breath and his tiny nose and whiskers would twitch. The little rat would be almost cute if I didn't know it was Cliff. "And that's what he turned into."

Daniel whistled through his teeth. "Well, at least he's not the hulking beast anymore. I can't tell you how many slaughtered animals I've come across in the last few days, how many families I've had to reassure. I wanted this thing caught as much as anyone. And then there's the fact that Beth is safe, too. That all of you are safe."

"Yeah, it's the best ending we could have hoped for," I muttered.

"What about the witch's body?" He asked.

"I think the police decided to tell everyone that a mountain lion came out of nowhere and killed her. I don't know if anyone will buy it but that's the story we're going with and would explain all the random animal deaths around town."

He shook his head. "Good. Although the sheriff must have grown a liking to you, because he knows about all this supernatural stuff, but he doesn't usually like to be involved in it." He grimaced at the garbage can. "And I can take care of that."

"Oh, I'm relieved. I hoped you'd be able to. I wasn't really sure what I was going to do if you didn't know what to do with him." I laid my head back on his couch and sighed.

"Hey, um, so I got a call from the sheriff," Daniel said carefully.

"Oh? Tonight?" Lifting my head, I tried to be casual.

"No, earlier. He said that your local PD called here to check up on you. Apparently, your ex is missing, along with his new lady friend."

I tried to act surprised. "Oh, no. Do they have any idea what's going on?"

It felt weird to hide the truth from Daniel, but he was still working with the police. If I told him what I'd done, he'd either have to get me in trouble or lie for me. And I didn't know how all of that would go. Were there specific punishments for the supernatural? Judges and juries? I'd have to ask the ladies. But for now, I didn't want to put him in a difficult position. Especially since I planned to address the issue anyway.

After a second of Daniel studying me, he continued, "They're not sure what's going on. They wanted to talk to me to see if I thought you'd have anything to do with it." He shook his head. "I told them it wasn't possible."

I was careful not to directly lie, and even though this was

the perfect opportunity to fess up, I couldn't bring myself to say the words. "That's crazy. Do you think they'll want to talk to me?"

Daniel nodded. "If they don't find your ex, I'd say so."

The mood in the cabin had darkened with the mention of my toad ex. I stretched and stood. "Well, I should be going, I suppose."

"Yeah, of course," he said, sounding uncertain.

I went to the door, opened it, and forced myself to walk out onto the porch. It felt like every instinct inside of me was screaming to stay longer, to just enjoy my time with Daniel for a few more minutes. But another part of me knew that might lead down the wrong road, and I wasn't ready for that yet.

"Before you go, I wanted to ask…"

I turned, feeling nervous. "Yes?"

"Would you like to go to dinner sometime?" Daniel leaned against the door jamb, looking the most awkward I've ever seen him, like he didn't quite know what to do with himself. "Or maybe I could cook for you?"

I wanted to scream yes, but I had to tie up some things with my ex first. "I think we could maybe set something up. Call me."

There. Now it was a little up in the air still and didn't feel so final.

## 25

## Emma

I WAS WHISTLING, ACTUALLY WHISTLING WHEN I GOT OUT OF my car back home. Was it weird to think of my parents' old house as more of a home than the one I'd lived in with Rick and Travis? Sure, I'd grown up here, but it was different living in it as an adult. Still, there was something comforting about it that I appreciated after everything that had happened.

Yeah, it was true that it'd been a heck of a last few days, but everything seemed to be coming together. I'd deal with my ex and his girlfriend, with my friends by my side, tie up my life back in Springfield, and settle back in at Mystic Hollow. Then, I'd go on a date with Daniel. And, I had a feeling, one date would turn into two and then three, until we were just together. Or that was what I hoped at least.

Maybe I was being silly. Hopelessly romantic. A few months ago, I would have called myself an idiot for even considering trusting another man, but now it felt as if everything I'd ever gone through was always leading to this moment.

It was the most certain I had ever felt about anything, other than my love for my son.

Pulling out my keys, I lifted them to the lock and froze. A note was taped to my door. My whistling died a swift death on my lips. My hand shook as I reached out for the note.

Maybe it was just a neighbor, reminding me to trim my shrubs. Or my brother, telling me to be quiet when I came home. There were a thousand things it could be.

But when I open it, I see the familiar writing.

You did *a bad thing to your husband and his lover. Karma comes for everyone.*

I felt sick. Not knowing what else to do, I texted my friends, telling them about the note. All the while, I was glancing around my darkened streets, looking for the culprit who was turning my life upside down. Fortunately, or unfortunately, the entire street was silent. Only the lonely wind kept me company.

A second later, a text came in from Deva. *It looks like it's time to end this thing, once and for all.*

My teeth clenched together. She was right. No one was going to keep me scared. No one was going to ruin the new life I'd worked so hard for. Whoever this note person was, whatever they wanted, once I dealt with Rick, they'd have nothing to hold over me.

I'd be truly free.

Crumpling the note in my fist, I glared out at the street. Karma was officially pissed.

. . .

Dɪᴅ ʏᴏᴜ ᴇɴᴊᴏʏ ᴛʜɪs ʙᴏᴏᴋ? **Then preorder your copy of Karma's Spirit.**

# ALSO BY L.A. BORUFF

PRIME TIME OF LIFE HTTPS://LABORUFF.COM/BOOKS/
PRIMETIME-OF-LIFE/
   *Borrowed Time*
   *Stolen Time*
   *Just in Time*

GIRDLES AND GHOULS HTTPS://WWW.BOOKS2READ.COM/
GIRDLES

WITCHING AFTER FORTY HTTPS://LABORUFF.COM/BOOKS/
WITCHING-AFTER-FORTY/
   *A Ghoulish Midlife*
   *Cookies For Satan (A Christmas Story)*
   *I'm With Cupid (A Valentine's Day Story)*
   *A Cursed Midlife*
   *Feeding Them Won't Make Them Grow (A Birthday Story)*
   *A Girlfriend For Mr. Snoozleton* (A Girlfriend Story)
   *A Haunting Midlife*

*An Animated Midlife*
*A Killer Midlife*

FANGED AFTER FORTY HTTPS://WWW.BOOKS2READ.COM/
FANGED1

*Bitten in the Midlife*

MAGICAL MIDLIFE in Mystic Hollow https://laboruff.com/
books/mystic-hollow/

*Karma's Spell*
*Karma's Shift*
*Karma's Spirit*

SHIFTING INTO MIDLIFE HTTPS://LABORUFF.COM/BOOKS/
SHIFTING-INTO-MIDLIFE/

*Pack Bunco Night*

# ABOUT L.A. BORUFF

L.A. (LAINIE) BORUFF LIVES IN EAST TENNESSEE WITH HER husband, three children, and an ever growing number of cats. She loves reading, watching TV, and procrastinating by browsing Facebook. L.A.'s passions include vampires, food, and listening to heavy metal music. She once won a Harry Potter trivia contest based on the books and lost one based on the movies. She has two bands on her bucket list that she still hasn't seen: AC/DC and Alice Cooper. Feel free to send tickets.

## ALSO BY LACEY CARTER ANDERSEN

**Guild of Assassins**

Mercy's Revenge

Mercy's Fall

**Monsters and Gargoyles**

Medusa's Destiny *audiobook*

Keto's Tale

Celaeno's Fate

Cerberus Unleashed

Lamia's Blood

Shade's Secret

Hecate's Spell

Empusa's Hunger

Shorts: Their Own Sanctuary

Shorts: Their Miracle Pregnancy

**Dark Supernaturals**

Wraith Captive

Marked Immortals

Chosen Warriors

**Wicked Reform School/House of Berserkers**

Untamed: Wicked Reform School

Unknown: House of Berserkers

Unstable: House of Berserkers

**Royal Fae Academy**

Revere (A Short Prequel)

Ravage

Ruin

Reign

Box Set: Dark Fae Queen

**Immortal Hunters MC**

Van Helsing Rising

Van Helsing Damned

**Magical Midlife in Mystic Hollow**

Karma's Spell

Karma's Shift

**Infernal Queen**

Raising Hell

Fresh Hell

Straight to Hell

**Her Demon Lovers**

Secret Monsters

Unchained Magic

Dark Powers

Box Set: Mate to the Demon Kings

**An Angel and Her Demons**

Supernatural Lies

Immortal Truths

Lover's Wrath

Box Set: Fallen Angel Reclaimed

**Legacy of Blood and Magic**

Dragon Shadows

Dragon Memories

**Legends Unleashed**

Don't Say My Name

Don't Cross My Path

Don't Touch My Men

**The Firehouse Feline**

Feline the Heat

Feline the Flames

Feline the Burn

Feline the Pressure

**God Fire Reform School**

Magic for Dummies

Myths for Half-Wits

Mayhem for Suckers

Box Set: God Fire Academy

**The Icelius Reverse Harem**

Her Alien Abductors

Her Alien Barbarians

Her Alien Mates

Collection: Her Alien Romance

**Steamy Tales of Warriors and Rebels**

Gladiators

**The Dragon Shifters' Last Hope**

Claimed by Her Harem

Treasured by Her Harem

Collection: Magic in her Harem

**Harem of the Shifter Queen**

Sultry Fire

Sinful Ice

Saucy Mist

Collection: Power in her Kiss

**Standalones**

Worthy (A Villainously Romantic Retelling)

Beauty with a Bite

Shifters and Alphas

**Collections**

Monsters, Gods, Witches, Oh My!

Wings, Horns, and Shifters

# ABOUT LACEY CARTER ANDERSEN

Lacey Carter Andersen is a USA Today bestselling author who loves reading, writing, and drinking excessive amounts of coffee. She spends her days taking care of her husband, three kids, and three cats. But at night, everything changes! Her imagination runs wild with strong-willed characters, unique worlds, and exciting plots that she enthusiastically puts into stories.

Lacey has dozens of tales: science fiction romances, paranormal romances, short romances, reverse harem romances, and more. So, please feel free to dive into any of her worlds; she loves to have the company!

And you're welcome to reach out to her; she really enjoys hearing from her readers.

You can find her at:

Email: laceycarterandersen@gmail.com

Mailing List:

https://www.subscribepage.com/laceycarterandersen

Website: https://laceycarterandersen.net/

Facebook Page: https://www.facebook.com/authorlaceycarterandersen

Manufactured by Amazon.ca
Bolton, ON